I0568018

Brand had completed his years of Service and was now a wealthy independent marked man. He was only thinking about taking a vacation and trying to figure out what was next for him when Sam floated into his life.

Sam is unlike any man Brand has ever met. Their relationship is unable to even get started because of Sam's obligation to his little brother, who is also marked like Brand. Together they seek answers to questions that not everyone wants them to ask. Will the obvious differences between Sam and Brand come between them, or will they find a way to make the relationship stay afloat?

The unauthorized reproduction or distribution of this copyrighted work is illegal. Criminal copyright infringement, including infringement without monetary gain, is investigated by the FBI and is punishable by up to 5 years in federal prison and a fine of $250,000.

This book is a work of fiction. Names, characters, places, and incidents either are products of the author's imagination or are used fictitiously. Any resemblance to actual events or locales or persons, living or dead, is entirely coincidental.

Rusty Cage
Copyright © 2019 Crawford Rhine
ISBN: 978-1-4874-2643-9
Cover art by Martine Jardin

All rights reserved. Except for use in any review, the reproduction or utilization of this work in whole or in part in any form by any electronic, mechanical or other means, now known or hereafter invented, is forbidden without the written permission of the publisher.

Published by eXtasy Books Inc or
Devine Destinies, an imprint of eXtasy Books Inc

Look for us online at:
www.eXtasybooks.com or www.devinedestinies.com

Rusty Cage
The Master & Servant Series
Book 8

By

Crawford Rhine

CHAPTER ONE

I had reached the end of my contract. My original contract had been extended twice and I was finishing my sixth year as a Servant to my Master. It had been a good six years and I had learned a lot, been a lot of places, blown a lot of cock, been fucked a lot, and made a lot of money.

When I turned thirteen years old, I had received my mark. It was a light blue mark that ran down my jaw line from my ear to my chin. The mark separated me from the other men in my world, who were known as NOMARs or non-marked men. Marked men were different from NOMARs because they were sexually attracted to men. Non-marked men were sexually attracted to women, which had long ago been separated from us.

The mark allowed me to have an opportunity that NOMARS didn't. Marked men could enter The Service, if they chose to. The Service was an organization that provided sexual Servants to wealthy NOMARs. If you entered The Service, they would pair you with a wealthy and potentially famous NOMAR to be your Master for a period of a year that could be continued if agreed upon by both parties. In exchange for one's Service, the NOMAR agreed to pay the Servant a million dollars a year.

In order to prepare marked guys for their life in Service, a series of training academies or schools had been established to teach us what we would need to know. These were called Service Academies, or SAs, and I entered mine when I was fifteen. Most NOMARs called them Sex Academies. I went to school there for three years before I was called to The Service by my Master.

I had just turned eighteen when I entered the ceremonial cage to be delivered to my Master. He lived in Boston, but he was semi-retired and travelled to different houses and hotels around the world for much of the year. His name was Patrick and he was forty-five when I first met him. He was kind and gentle with me, which was far better treatment than some of the Servants received from *their* Masters.

Patrick was very wealthy, either from investments or inheritance, I was never quite sure, but we had a great time together. I wasn't really attracted to him physically, but I liked him as a friend and so therefore, it wasn't difficult for me to pleasure him on a regular basis. Plus, he was paying me a lot of fucking money that would make me financially secure for the rest of my life.

After a couple weeks into Service with Patrick, he revealed his favorite facet of his sex life to me. We were out to lunch at a local bar-b-que dive and were seated at a picnic table on the porch. Patrick constantly surprised me with how down-to-earth he was for such a rich person, and there was never a place or activity that he wasn't willing to try. I had always assumed that rich people were snobs, but Patrick constantly proved me wrong.

We placed our orders and were waiting for our food when a group of four guys came in and sat at the picnic table beside us. They were probably construction workers, based on their clothing—tank tops, jeans, and steel-toed work boots. One man stood out to me. He was older, with a full white beard and a salt-and-pepper flat top. He was a physical specimen, not only because his muscles rippled under his tank top, but because they were completely covered in tattoos. Neither the muscles nor the tats seemed to go with the white beard, and I noticed that he had kind eyes and nice teeth. Much like

Patrick, he seemed to be someone that I was trying to put into a box, but couldn't.

I turned and saw that Patrick was also admiring or at least sizing-up the group beside us. He turned back with a neutral face and asked me where we might like to vacation at the end of the month. It was exciting for me to be with someone who was so well-versed in travel and had the means to go anywhere he wanted for as long as he wanted. I was thrilled that he was treating me with respect and was letting me pick where we could vacation. I loved to travel and had a big wish list, so at the time, my head swam with all the possibilities.

Our food came and we talked excitedly about different exotic locations. I would mention a place and Patrick would tell me his experiences in that locale. When we were almost finished eating, Patrick excused himself to the restroom, and I watched the men at the other table and eavesdropped on their conversation. I was shocked to see after a minute or so that Patrick had walked by and stopped at their table. He was talking to the tatted man and nodded at me with his head.

The big man looked over at me and smiled easily. I wasn't sure what was going on, but I smiled back, noticing that all of the men were looking at me now. Patrick talked with him for a few more seconds and then put something down on the table in front of him. My Master returned to our table, and I was dying to know what was going on. The SA had taught me many things—how to protect myself, how to pleasure a man in many ways, how to cook, how to be respectful at all times—but the one thing they taught me how to do that really irritated me was to keep quiet until I was prompted to speak. This was one of those times.

Patrick used my training to his advantage now, not bringing up his visit to the other table and letting me suffer. He picked up the check and we headed out of the restaurant without a word. In the car, he asked me about what I might want to do tomorrow, but said nothing about what had just happened. I let it go, since I was powerless to find out. We went shopping for vacation clothes for me, and Patrick spent a tremendous amount of money on me.

We returned home, and Patrick's butler, Rich, unloaded our purchases while his chef, Bolton, served our dinner in the dining room. I was thrilled to have been placed with such a man that could live this way, and I had promised myself not to screw it up. There were many stories of Masters who abused, degraded, or just down-right tortured their Servants, so I was thankful for Patrick every minute of the day. At the end of the dinner, the doorbell rang, and Rich answered it.

"Mr. McCrae for you, sir," Rich said as he escorted someone into the dining room.

Patrick and I stood up, since we were finished with dinner anyway, and I saw that it was the construction guy from the bar-b-que joint. Needless to say, I was stunned to see him — here.

"Ah, Mr. McCrae. Nice to see you again," Patrick said, as he extended his hand. "This is Brand, my Servant."

I held out my hand to shake his. I was amazed at how the visitor's big hand engulfed mine. It was rough and hot to the touch and I immediately felt the burn start in my crotch that signaled my desire. "Nice to meet you."

"Likewise," he said in a deep voice.

"Well, why don't we retire upstairs?" Patrick led the way, talking small talk with McCrae as we climbed the stairs and went into the spare bedroom. I knew from having explored the house that this bedroom was for guests and contained a king-sized bed. Patrick and I slept in the Master bedroom across the hall.

"Mr. McCrae, there is a restroom right here. If you would like to wash up, I will let Brand know of our plans."

McCrae didn't say anything, but went into the restroom

and closed the door behind him.

"Brand, I would like Mr. McCrae to fuck you while I watch."

I swallowed hard. This was a command, even though it was stated as a desire, and I was powerless to do anything about it . . . as if I would anyway. "Yes, sir."

"I could tell you were intrigued by him at the restaurant, and I didn't think you would mind doing this for me."

"No, sir."

"Excellent. Now, let's give him the time of his life, huh?"

I smiled at Patrick's enthusiasm, saying, "Yes, sir."

McCrae came out of the bathroom and was unsure of what to do next. I walked over to him, took him by the hand and led him to the bed. Sitting down on the edge of the bed, I put him in front of me and lifted the bottom of his tank top until it went up and over his head. I ran my hand down his chiseled tattooed chest, pinching his nipples as I came to them.

McCrae made a sound somewhere between gasping and snorting as I pinched his sensitive nubbins.

I checked on my Master, who had pulled a Queen Anne chair up to the end of the bed, sat down in it, and crossed his legs. His eyes were alight with interest.

I looked up into McCrae's eyes. They were alight, too, with desire, as he stared down at me. Looking back down, I unbuckled his belt. I unzipped his zipper before unbuttoning the waist. Reaching inside his open fly, I grabbed his cock inside. It was already really hard and hot, pressed against the inside of his boxers. He was big and I was afraid if I tried to pull that big monster out of his fly that I might hurt him so I settled for feeling him up.

"Oh, fuck," McCrae uttered through clenched teeth as I massaged his hard-on. I pulled my hand out and pushed on his jeans. They fell to his ankles and I pushed the waistband of his boxers after them.

The construction worker's cock popped out of his boxers all by itself, in all of its glory. It was thick and longer than average, arching out of a bush of copper-colored hair. Wondering why his drapes didn't match the carpet, I looked up at him and smiled. I wasn't sure if the normal sex talk was appropriate in this situation with my Master a few feet away. I didn't want to hurt Patrick's feelings by commenting on how big McCrae was or anything.

I decided to keep it to myself and instead I held McCrae's gaze with mine as I lowered my head and licked his hot cock from its root to its tip. McCrae opened his mouth, but no words were able to escape. I flicked my tongue over the velvety-soft head and was rewarded by a single drop of delicious pre-cum. I caught it on the tip of my tongue. I think it was almost more than he could take, and I felt his need increase in intensity.

Putting McCrae out of his misery, I grabbed both of his hips and swallowed his substantial member. He tasted like sweat and man-musk. I swallowed all the way until my nose was buried in his pubic hair, held there, and breathed in deeply of his scent.

"God damn!" McCrae said. "I can't believe this is happening to me."

I pulled back to see that McCrae was directing his comments to my Master. I started to piston up and down on his big cock, enjoying more pre-cum that he produced as I worked. I felt his rough hands on the sides of my short-shaven hair.

"I'm gonna fucking come!" he yelled hoarsely.

I bore down on his cock, not letting up at all as he reached his climax. McCrae roared as he held my head and shot a big load of salty hot cum into my mouth. I swallowed it down to keep from choking. He tasted good, and I liked that he continued to face-fuck me through his climax.

When he finally slowed, I set to work on licking his shaft and balls, getting all of his cum into my mouth and down my gullet. I hoped he wasn't sated yet, because I had more in store for him. Standing up, I ran my hands up his chest again, grabbing his big biceps and turning him around so that we switched places. McCrae had a look of complete awe on his face that changed to surprise when I pushed him down onto the bed.

Kneeling in front of him, I began to unlace his boots. I took them off one at a time, making sure that I smelled his heady foot odor for each, and then pulled his jeans and boxers off. His legs weren't as muscular as his arms, but they were covered in fine copper hair and the occasional tattoo. I stood up and undressed in front of him, never breaking eye contact with him. He propped himself up on those gorgeous arms to be able to see me better.

I gave McCrae quite a show of slowly removing all of my clothes, making sure he got more than an eyeful of my ass. When I was completely naked, I checked with my Master, saw his small head nod, and then climbed on top of McCrae. I straddled his big body at his waist, sucking his nipples on the way. I reached behind me and grabbed his cock, pleased to see that he was hard again. The bottle of lube I needed was on the nightstand, so I shifted my body weight to get it. Squirting lube on my hand, I reached back and slicked up his hard member as he watched my every move.

"Do you want to be inside me, McCrae?" I asked him seductively.

He licked his lips under his beard and stach. "Yeah." His voice was gruff with need and desire.

"Would you like to see where you want to be?"

His voice broke as he said, "Yeah."

I stepped over him and onto all fours on the bed with my ass pointed right at his head. He propped himself back up on one elbow, and I felt his rough fingers on my ass. McCrae was exploring my backside, and his cock twitched in anticipation. I twisted back and squirted lube on his big outstretched fingers. At first, I thought he didn't know why I had done that, but then comprehension must have hit him, because he wiped my little puckered hole with the lube.

"Push it in, McCrae," I commanded him.

He hesitated at first, but then a big rough finger pushed through my anal ring and buried itself to the hilt inside of me. I gasped as he moved it around and then inserted a second one inside me. He worked his fingers like a cock, plunging them in and then pulling them almost all the way out.

"Amazing," he said, almost to himself.

I leaned forward, pulling myself off his fingers. With one hand on his chest, I pushed him back flat onto the bed. Straddling him again, I moved his slick cock into position against my rosebud.

"Are you sure it will go in?" McCrae asked innocently.

I tried not to roll my eyes. "I'm sure it will," I told him as I cut my eyes at my Master, who was chuckling silently. "You ready?"

McCrae nodded his head and placed his rough hands on the sides of my chest. I pushed back onto his cock and felt the head pop through my anal ring as it stretched around his fat shaft. McCrae's mouth formed an *O* shape as I continued to push back and down, letting more of his cock slide into me.

When I hit the bottom, I wiggled around so that every possible inch of him was inside me and I was sitting on his nest of pubic hair. Now it was McCrae's turn to run his hands up and down my chest.

I needed to be still for a moment, because McCrae was the biggest piece of meat I'dhad fuck me since The Service Academy, so I was experiencing more than a little bit of pain. Sharp red tongues of pain coursed through my body, but as I calmed my breathing and relaxed, they soon turned to purple waves of pleasure. The stabbing pain went away and the wonderful feeling of fullness McCrae was giving me replaced it.

"Fuck, that's the tightest little ass I've ever been in," McCrae crowed.

"Thanks. Now do you think you can give that tight little ass a good fucking, or not?" I challenged him.

"Hell yeah!"

Elevated slightly above his crotch, I held onto his biceps as he reached back, held my butt cheeks apart, and started to fuck up into me. It was a good fuck, and his fat cock was giving my ass hole a good stretch with each thrust. We both started to sweat from the efforts of our activity, and after a while, I stopped him.

Whispering into his ear, I asked, "Wanna watch that big cock destroying my tiny ass?" I knew he would.

"Yes, please," he whimpered.

I smiled to myself and stood up off of him. I got back onto all fours in the middle of the bed and he kneeled behind me. McCrae slid his fat cock back inside me, watching it go all the way inside me. He planted his big hands on my lower back and pulled me back further onto his cock.

"Oh yeah." McCrae started fucking with a strong pace, slamming into me and pulling me back onto him as I drifted forward. It was a great fuck and I buried my head into the pillows as his giant ball sack swung with each stroke and slapped my own. He built to his climax quickly and then roared again as he flooded my ass with his hot seed.

McCrae was breathing heavily as he held his cock inside of me and wrapped his big arms around my waist, hugging me to him.

"That was hot, McCrae. Thanks," I said to him.

"Do you think you can go once more, Mr. McCrae?"

Master's voice shocked me because it was so close. I looked up, and he was standing next to the bed. I couldn't see McCrae's face, but I bet it was shocked also.

"Yes, sir," I heard McCrae say.

"Good. I know Brand would like you to fuck him in the Missionary position before you go."

It was my favorite position, and my cock got hard just thinking of McCrae's weight pressing me down into the mattress. My Master knew my body and knew what I liked.

"No problem," McCrae mumbled as he pulled his hips back and his cock popped out of my hole, leaving me feeling empty all of a sudden.

I turned around and cleaned his dick up for him. I licked his hot cum off his fuck-stick. I continued to lick it, even after he was clean, until he was hard again. I pulled my mouth off him and stroked him with my hand while I flipped over onto my back, lifting my legs. I didn't have to direct McCrae, who saw his target and wasted no time getting to it.

"I can't believe my fucking luck," he said as I put my ankles onto his broad shoulders and he pointed his hard cock at my hole.

"I think I might be the lucky one, McCrae."

"You like this cock inside you?" He pushed it in just as he asked and I arched my back as he slammed into me. McCrae bent me in half, held himself up on his big arms, and walked his legs forward, lifting my ass up higher and letting him sink deeper into me.

"Fuck me." I sighed as he held me there, impaled on his giant tool.

"Okay," he mumbled as he begun to fucking destroy my ass. I grabbed ahold of his big biceps and held on as he rocked me back and forth, fucking my ass like his life depended on it. I was a little embarrassed to be getting so thoroughly rocked in front of Patrick, but there was nothing I could do about it, because my body was responding to this fucking and McCrae was pushing all of my buttons.

I moaned out loud as his cock punched my prostate time and again. McCrae increased his speed and plowed a furrow into my ass. His sweat dripped down his big chest and plopped like giant raindrops onto my stomach. He was starting to make small grunting noises with each thrust, and I could feel his cock throb inside me, indicating that he was close to his explosion. I squeezed him with my ass muscles, sending him into a fit of physical spasms as he hit his climax and busted his nut.

I hit my climax with him, spurting threads of white-hot ropy spunk across my stomach and chest. I arched my back and rode out the sensations that were pulsing through our bodies, the only thing registering in my mind was the fact that McCrae was continuing to fuck through his climax, even though it was his third in the past hour. I was quite impressed with him.

"God damn!" McCrae exploded as he slowed down.

"Rich, please come up and escort Mr. McCrae out." Looking over, I saw that Patrick was talking on his cell phone. He hung up and said, "Mr. McCrae, I can't thank you enough for your services. My man will have a cash gift for you to show my appreciation."

"Jesus. This sweet piece of tail *and* cash?" McCrae looked like he was in shock as he pulled out of me, crawled off the bed and started to get dressed. He turned back towards me and awkwardly said, "Um, thanks, Brand."

I smiled as I brought my legs up to my chest and watched McCrae getting dressed, "No, thank you, McCrae."

Rich came to pick up McCrae, who waved at us from the doorway before leaving. Master finally stood up, and I realized that he was sporting an incredible hard-on. He approached the bed and we spent an amazing night together.

That was when I knew that my Master liked to watch. We spent the next two years in much the same manner — me getting fucking tore up by a variety of men who were very different from my Master and then getting fucked even harder by Patrick after they left. At the end of the two-year contract, Patrick and I agreed to extend it two more years and at the end of that one, we agreed on one last extension.

Patrick had been very good to me and had introduced me to all the best food, locations, people, clothes, and style. He had also given me four million dollars. Four . . . million . . . dollars. I still couldn't believe it. Patrick had also taught me how to invest and how to keep money once I had it, so I felt like anything was possible. Probably the greatest gift he gave me was that he had invested my money for me, even before my time with him was up, so that when it was up, I was a wealthy, wealthy man.

"What will you do, now that it is all over?" Patrick asked me.

"I'm not sure. I want to go on vacation for a while, to the beach that my family used to go to every year in South Carolina. It will give me time to try to figure out what I want to do."

"That's smart. Do you think you will go to Pittsburgh like you had always planned to?"

"Probably. At least at first. Thanks for everything you did for me, Patrick, and for treating me so well."

"My pleasure. I will have your things shipped to you wherever you finally settle, and I have a gift for you for your new house."

"Master —"

He interrupted me. "Patrick, now."

"Patrick. You have given me so much already."

"It's not much." He walked over to a square with fabric draped over it. With a flourish he removed the fabric and revealed my cage. "I had it made into a coffee table for the man-cave in your new house. Do you like it?"

"Oh, Patrick," I gushed as I hugged him. "I love it." Running my hands over the smooth wooden top, I thought back to all of those years ago when I arrived in it. I had had a lot of experiences since then, and I was thrilled to start a whole lot of new ones.

CHAPTER TWO

Ocean Drive was exactly as I remembered it, except for a few new high-rise condos that had gone up along the ocean. The rented BMW sports car I was driving purred as I cruised down the main drag at twenty-five miles per hour. I had rented a house for two weeks on the beachfront between Cherry Grove and Ocean Drive, where the really big mansions were located. My dad, brothers, and I used to drive by them and marvel at the idea that anyone could own something so big. Now, thanks to the internet, I could see that some of them had been torn down and rebuilt in modern splendor. I selected the most expensive one for rent and reserved it.

Walking into the realty company office, I enjoyed the looks from the employees and from the other renters waiting to check in. I knew that a marked man was a pretty rare sight, and that day I enjoyed the stares.

When I gave my name to the receptionist, the owner practically jumped across the desk trying to get to me. I didn't enjoy this fawning that regular people did over the rich, and I wouldn't indulge it. I waited my turn behind the other families, much to the owner's consternation. When it was finally my turn, I signed the contract and accepted the key. They asked if I needed directions, and I enjoyed their looks of disbelief as I informed them that I was very familiar with the area already.

I drove to the house and unpacked my bags. I had rented this sports car for the two weeks, but I would need to shop for one of my own as soon as I decided where I was going to put my roots down. Patrick was kind enough to let me keep all the electronics he had given to me during my Service, so I didn't need a lot in that department. I had called Verizon and had my own account set up and my phone transferred to it. I didn't want to be beholden to Patrick any more than I already was.

The beach house was absolutely stunning. Right on the beach with sand dunes between its large porch and the ocean, it was a modern marvel. Everything was brand new and the top of the line. Patrick would have been proud. I unpacked my suitcases and put everything away. Changing clothes, I headed out to the grocery store. I got more than a few stares in the Bi-Lo at the beach, but enjoyed shopping for food for the first time in six years. After all those years of letting Patrick or his employees do everything for me, it all seemed fresh and new, and I wondered how long it would be before I burned out on this new honeymoon phase of my post-Service life.

On the way home from the store, I wondered what the old place looked like now where we stayed as kids. I took a hard right turn on Hillside Drive to see. As I approached Sixteenth Avenue, I saw that the three big old houses on the corner that had always rented to college and high school kids were still in swing. There seemed to be close to twenty guys in the yard, drinking and hanging out. One particularly hot young guy caught my eye as he leaned against one of the house stilts. He had a full head of black hair and board shorts on. His chest was very muscular, but thin with black hair outlining his nipples and his treasure trail. He nodded his head at me as I stopped at the stop sign.

In the block in front of me were the old condos, which were called Waipani. They looked the same as I remembered, except instead of the dark grey wood it was now a brighter stucco color. The pool looked inviting and I told myself that I would come down for a swim sometime soon. I pulled the BMW back onto Hillside Drive and stopped at the stop sign. I looked for the guy propped on the stilt, but didn't see him.

"This is a nice car."

I jumped at the voice right next to my open car window. I looked over, and it was the guy with the nice chest. He had grabbed the roof and was looking inside.

"Wanna go for a ride?" I asked as my heart rate decreased slightly.

"Sure." He opened the passenger-side door and jumped inside.

"I'm Brand," I said as I held out my hand.

"Brock," he said, as he took my hand and shook it.

I made the turn and then the next onto Ocean Drive. The speed limit was really low here, but the ocean breeze blowing through the car was wonderful. "So, you down here for graduation, Brock?"

"Yeah, me and my buddies from school are staying at that house."

"What school?"

"Elon." I knew it to be a small college in North Carolina somewhere in the middle of the state.

"Cool. Hey, you wanna drive?" I turned to look into his face.

"Are you kidding? Of course I do!" I pulled over on one of the side streets and switched places with him. In front of the car as we exchanged places, he looked at me straight in the face for the first time. "Thanks, dude . . ." His voice faltered as he gazed on the light blue mark on the side of my face for the first time.

We got back in the car and Brock put on his seatbelt turning to me and said, "You're marked."

"Yes."

He swallowed hard and said, "Cool." Brock shifted into gear and took off. After we had driven on the bypass highway for a while, he slowed the car down to merge back onto Highway 17.

"So are you like a Servant or something?" he asked cautiously.

"Not anymore."

"Really? You rich?" His youth was showing.

"What do you think?"

"I'm thinking *yes*."

I didn't like this line of questioning, so I attempted to change the topic. "I'm thinking that I'm hungry. You?"

"I could eat and have a beer."

"There's a drive-in down the block." He turned the car and pulled in. We ordered from the speaker and sat back listening to the radio.

"So, what was it like?" Brock finally asked.

I was ready for this question, but decided to make him squirm a bit. "What was what like?"

He got very nervous. "You know, being a Servant."

"It was one big fucking cock right after another," I said plainly, seeing that the blow landed, shocking him.

"Dude."

"Sorry. It was good, you know . . . he was nice to me."

He was nervously tapping the steering wheel and he was cutting his eyes to look at me without seeming to. "Did you have to do all kinds of freaky things?"

The food came and Brock downed his beer.

"No, but I did them anyway."

Brock made a motion like he might spit up his beer, but kept it down.

"Sorry, dude," I said, laughing and using his vocabulary.

Brock started to laugh and we toasted to that before digging in to our burgers. After we finished the food, I paid the bill and we switched places. Brock reached in his shorts and pulled a pack of cigarettes out.

"You mind if I smoke?"

I looked at him and said, "Wouldn't you rather fuck?"

He sputtered, looking to see if I was serious or not. "What?"

"You heard me. Let me know what you want to do, so I know where to drive to. I don't fuck guys who smoke."

"I'll fuck."

"I thought you might. How old are you, Brock?"

"Nineteen. You?"

"Twenty-four." I pulled into the driveway of my beach house.

"Holy fuck! Is this your place?"

"Yeah, man."

"It's fucking awesome!"

"Thanks." I unlocked the door and we climbed up to the great room with the groceries. The views of the setting sun's light on the ocean were awesome and I got us a beer from the grocery bags. Putting some of the food in the fridge, I noticed that Brock was checking the porch out. I remembered what Patrick had taught me and locked my keys and wallet in the safe that was provided in this rental house.

When Brock came back in from the porch, I pushed him onto one of the leather sofas and sucked his nipples while I undid his board shorts, pulling them down his legs.

"Fuck . . ." He breathed heavily.

Brock wasn't wearing anything under his shorts, and his cock popped out right in front of my face as I pulled his shorts down. It was the typical young man's cock — skinny, long, and hard as a rock. I stroked it with my thumb on the big bottom vein before engulfing him with my mouth. Brock tasted like he had jacked off that morning and was also salty from the ocean. I pistoned up and down on his hard member, sucking his pre-cum down as fast as he could produce it. I sucked so hard that my cheeks were hollowed out by the action.

I felt his cock twitch in my mouth as I pulled on his balls and knew that he was close to his climax. I increased my pace and continued to blow him as he exploded inside me. Brock's youthful cum tasted sweet and delicious. He coated the back of my mouth with hard shots of spunk that I swallowed down in order not to choke.

"Jesus Christ!" Brock blurted out.

I pulled his cock out of my mouth and cleaned it up by licking it from the root to the head between my lips. "Very nice, Brock." I sat back on my heels and took another big swig of beer. "Is that the first time you've ever been blown by a marked guy?"

"Yeah...and it was fucking awesome!" He finished his beer and sat it down. "A neighbor kid sucked my dick once when I was young, but he turned out to be a NOMAR."

"Cocksucking NOMAR," I said, starting to laugh as I undressed.

Brock laughed, too, and I saw that he was still hard. I crawled up onto the couch, straddling him, and sat on his waist. I grabbed a bottle of lube from the side table where I had cleverly placed it this afternoon. Squirting it in my hand, I slicked his already-wet cock and then my tiny puckered hole.

"You ready?" I asked him before pushing down and back, not waiting for his answer. Brock's cock split my anal ring and slid inside me. He didn't really do it for me, but he was fun to play with today, so I squeezed his cock with my ass muscles and pushed myself up off of him.

Brock groaned under me as I moved up and down on him. His voice was hoarse with need as he croaked, "Dude, that hole is insanely tight."

"Thanks, Brock."

"Weren't you a Servant for a few years?" he asked in disbelief.

"Yeah. What, you don't think a Servant can have a tight ass after serving his time?"

"I didn't think so, but God damn if I'm not wrong."

"Shut up and fuck me." I moaned as I held myself still elevated above him and let him jackhammer my ass from below. Brock was really talented at this and had the stamina of a nineteen-year-old. He seemed to fuck forever, my asshole burning from the friction before he buried in deeply and shot his second load.

"How's that?" Brock asked innocently like a kid asking how he rode his bike for the first time.

"Pretty good, Brock," I said, between gulps of air. I could see how this nineteen-year-old could wear me out if I would let him. I'd rested my head on his muscular chest and I didn't want him to think I was weak, so I asked him, "Wanna go again?"

His face lit up and he said, "Sure."

I stood up off him, his cock popping out of my ass. "Upstairs," I said as I nodded my head at the stairs. I headed that way and heard him follow behind me. Brock, like a puppy, was letting me lead him around, just as happy with letting me take the lead. This was not the guy for me, but it wouldn't stop me from having some fun with him.

I walked into the bedroom and heard Brock gasp, following behind me. The view of the ocean was stunning from the Master bedroom with a whole wall made of glass, affording every possible view.

"Man, this house is jacked!"

I wasn't even sure what that meant, but I thanked him anyway. Grabbing each of his wrists, I held his arms above his head and slammed him up against the wall. Brock's pulse increased and his breath caught in his throat. I knew that I had him totally mesmerized. Moving my face close to his, I bit his earlobe and then licked down his smooth-shaven cheek to his chin. I heard his breath catch. I continued to run my tongue down his thick throat and across his collarbone.

I had to release his wrists so that I could bend further down as I continued to lick a wet path to each of his nipples, which I bit and sucked on before proceeding down across his phenomenal abs.

"Christ! This is the hottest thing I have ever done," Brock said quickly, his voice heavy with lust.

"Shut up," I said as I flicked the tip of my tongue into his belly button and then continued down his treasure trail to his cock. I loved the taste of his cum on his cock. It was intoxicating to me as I slobbered over him, continually pushing him against the wall.

I sucked his young cock until he got hard again and began to moan. Squirting lube directly on his cock, I stroked him with my hand, feeling his temperature rise as I worked. Releasing him, I stepped back to the bed and climbed on it, lying down on my back. Brock followed me, climbing over me and lifting my legs up onto his shoulders. He used one hand to guide his cock to my hole again and then pushed past my anal ring.

Brock must have liked this missionary position, because he rose to the occasion, fucking me faster and deeper than before. I enjoyed watching his face as he plumbed my depths over and over, hitting my prostate repeatedly. I could see from his face that his climax was coming, minutes before it actually arrived. He growled through this climax, punching into me in staccato thrusts throughout it.

"Fuck me," he finally said, as he finished and rolled off me, both of us hot sweaty messes.

"I just did," I said, starting to laugh. "I'm going to shower and then I'll drive you home."

"Mind if I shower, too?"

I looked at him and decided he was being harmless instead of sexual and I told him to go for it. We both showered and redressed, talking about his future plans after college. He was planning on going into real estate, which Patrick would have surely admired.

Brock surprised me by saying, "You know, I can walk from here."

"Really?" I asked in disbelief.

"Yeah. My buddies will be cruising the strip in the back of a truck, so they'll only be a couple blocks from here. I'll call them as I walk."

"You sure?"

"Yeah. I had a great time though."

"Yeah, me, too."

"Can I swing by tomorrow?" he asked, his brown eyes wide like he was afraid of the answer.

"I don't think so, Brock." I saw the disappointment cross his face. Deciding to soften the blow, I added, "I know where I can find you though, right?"

"Yes, you do."

"Good luck, Brock."

"See ya!" he yelled as he descended the stairs.

I locked the front door, opened a bottle of beer, and headed out to the porch to sit in a rocking chair and listen to the sound of the surf, hoping tomorrow would be as good as today was.

CHAPTER THREE

The next morning, I fixed myself breakfast and went out onto the beach. I'd noticed from my bedroom window and then again from the great room that the beach in front of my house was completely empty. Having never been able to afford these big houses before, I did not realize that this was one of the drawbacks, or advantages, to living or renting here, depending on how you looked at it. I was a people person and my favorite thing to do at the beach, besides body surf, was people-watching.

Over breakfast, I decided to go down the beach closer to where we used to go, across from the Waipani condos. It would definitely be more crowded. I had slept in and taken time to get all of my supplies ready, so the beach was pretty crowded by the time I got there.

I set my chair in the soft gray sand near the edge of the water, where I knew I would be able to see a lot of people walking by. As soon as I had everything the way I wanted it, including screwing the damn umbrella stand into the sand, I headed for the water to cool off. It was colder than I remembered, but it was still early June. Once I dove under a few waves, the water felt fine to me.

The murky water and salty whitecaps brought back a ton of memories of my brothers and me playing in the surf. The waves were great, and I used them to body surf into the beach. I was out of practice, but it came back to me pretty quickly as I attempted one after another.

On one of the failed attempts, I came out of the wake of the wave and saw an inflatable boat coming towards me. The orange boat had moorings for oars, but I didn't see any. It held two men. One seemed to have a stunning body, although I couldn't really see his head. His feet were propped up on the sides of the boat, and they were large and flat, just like I like them. The boat shifted and I could see he was blond and very tan, almost golden.

And that was when I noticed the second guy. He was younger, maybe even ten years younger than the twenty-something golden God. And he was marked. I saw the light blue mark on his face just as a big wave slapped the back of my head and sent me underwater. When I came up, the boat had careened off down the beach and I lost sight of it.

Just as well. He already has a Servant. Figuring he was a rich kid whose family probably bought him a Servant, I rode another wave in and kept walking back to my chair. I was rewarded with quite a few slack-jawed looks as I came out of the water. Most people had not noticed my mark on the way in, but now they did. I tried to see if I could spot the orange inflatable boat on the sand anywhere, but I didn't see it.

I pulled out a magazine to read and a beer to drink and settled in for some people watching. The weather was great, not too hot, with a very nice breeze coming across the beach. There weren't a lot of great-looking men there at the moment, so I actually finished a whole magazine under the umbrella without any crude interruptions from men looking to get lucky. I decided to get some rays, so I reapplied my sunscreen and moved my chair down into the water to sit. There was a man there doing the same thing while his two young kids played in the water. I scanned the water for the orange boat, but it was still missing.

The dad said hello to me as I sat down and I gave him a quick greeting. He didn't strike me as anything special, but I did enjoy watching his kids splash around. Ten minutes later or so, the kids asked their dad to come out in the water with them. He looked around to see if he could move his chair anywhere.

"I'll watch it for you," I told him.

"Thanks. It looks like the tide is coming in, so I'll move it up here beside you."

"No problem," I said as I returned to my *Sports Illustrated*. The dad took off his sunglasses, hat, and Under Armor shirt and headed to the waves. I had to admit that he looked a hell of a lot better without his hat, glasses, and shirt. He was my height with a slightly thick body. He had blond hair that was cut really short, military-style. I scanned the water for the inflatable boat one more futile time before returning to a story on who might win the US Open.

"That's not really the magazine I would have thought you would be reading," a voice said above me.

I looked up, startled to see the dad standing beside me. "Pardon me?"

He looked embarrassed, suddenly. "The SI magazine. I just didn't pick you for a sports fan."

I noticed that he had a heavy shadow of a beard on his square jawed face, but only a soul patch showing. His eyes were blue with just a little red from the saltwater. "Why, because marked guys are pansies?"

My frankness caught him off-guard, like I had expected it to. "Well, no, I mean, yes, but . . ."

I shaded my eyes with my hand so I could really get a look at him. He was thick, but still muscular, like an ex-football player who had gotten older and let himself go a little. It was quite alluring, at least to me.

"I'm sorry. I didn't mean to offend you. You're just the first marked guy I ever met."

"I'm not offended. I'm just giving you a little down-country for thinking in those stereotypes. I'm Brand," I said as I extended my hand.

"Ken." He shook my hand with a big paw of his own and I felt the sexual chemistry between us as soon as I touched his skin.

"Your boys are cute, Ken."

"Thanks. They're having the time of their lives down here this week."

"I used to have the best time when I came down here as a kid, as well."

"Oh, yeah? Mind if I join you?" he asked, pointing at his chair.

"No, please. Where you from?"

"Ohio. Our first trip down as a family."

"Nice."

"Yeah, we're staying at the Mar Vista, right here."

"I know it." The Mar Vista had been a shitty little two-story hotel until recently, when they had sold out to a large corporation. It was now a twenty-five-story behemoth done in Italian style. I was sure it probably blocked the sun and the view from a whole block of houses and condos behind it.

Ken and I chatted for a while longer while we watched his boys play. He was a nice guy, and the boys were also, when I met them. They stared at my mark and asked their dad about it.

"Brand's just like you and me, except he is special," Ken told them. They accepted that and returned to the waves.

"That was nice of you, Ken," I said as I stared at him.

"Yeah? Well, it's true."

"Ken, I was planning on heading home to take a nap, but I wondered if you might like to go to dinner tonight . . . my treat."

He didn't know what to say, and I took his silence as a negative. "It's all right if you can't. You have the boys."

"No, it's not that. My dad is here and he can watch them. I

just can't believe that this is happening. I'm a little in shock."

"It's dinner, Ken," I said sarcastically.

"Oh, shit. I'm being stereotypical again, aren't I? I was just assuming that we were going to fuck afterwards," he admitted and began to chuckle, lightening up for the first time.

"Well, we are, aren't we?" I asked, starting to laugh, myself.

He burst out laughing and his laugh was contagious.

"Sometimes stereotypes are true," I told him as I handed him my card. It was another thing Patrick had taught me, to always carry a business card with me that just had my first name and cell number on it. I was glad I'd put some in a plastic baggie in the back of my chair. "Call me and let me know what time to pick you up." I stood up and grabbed my chair out of the sucking sand and water and carried it up to my umbrella. I gathered my things and left.

Getting back to the house, I took that nap and woke up refreshed. There was a message on my phone from Ken and a text from Patrick. I listened to Ken's message where he nervously said that he would meet me in front of the Mar Vista at six-thirty. Patrick's text asked how it was going and said that the house was lonely without me. Patrick and I had talked about whether he would replace me or not once I was gone. He wasn't sure and had decided to play it by ear.

I texted him back.

Are you ready for another Servant already?

What? Do you think I'm made of money?

Hahaha and yes!

I miss you

Miss you, too. The beach is really nice and bringing back a lot of fond memories from childhood

Cool

More later.

I'd showered when I got home from the beach, so all I had

to do was get dressed and shave. That didn't take long, so I turned on the TV and recorded a couple of shows that would be on tonight. I had been a huge TV fan before going into The Service, but Patrick didn't like TV, so it had been a long time since I had seen anything.

I walked out onto the porch to stare at the ocean. The humidity hit me as soon as I opened the French doors and I was glad I had picked a linen shirt for tonight's dinner. I locked the doors to the house and went down the back steps to the garage under the house to the car.

I arrived at the Mar Vista at exactly six-thirty and saw Ken waiting. He was nervously fidgeting with his clothes. He looked nice in dress shorts and a subtle Hawaiian shirt. I pulled over and he climbed inside the car.

"Hi," I said.

"Hey." He shut the door and put his seatbelt on.

"You nervous, Ken?"

"Yeah, a little bit," he admitted.

"I'm going to be very straightforward with you. I would like us to talk at dinner about our lives and then after dinner we will do whatever you are comfortable with. I would like to fuck with you, but I will leave it up to you, unless I decide at dinner that I am not interested in you." I pulled out into traffic.

He swallowed hard at my brutal honesty and at my words. "Okay. I've never met anyone who talks like you."

"You'll get used to it," I said with a snort. "What kind of food would you like to eat?"

"Anything. We've had seafood already a bunch." Ken's voice sounded less tense now and he looked more relaxed.

"I think I'm in the mood for a steak."

"Sounds good." Ken smiled. I headed to the Boundary House in Calabash. It was new, but I had read good reviews. The food was excellent, and Ken and I talked about his kids and my time in Service. I was really interested in how he had procured the kids—by sending his sperm to the Heir Service and waiting to see if it would be chosen by a female on their side of our world, as he explained. And then if the baby was a boy, it was sent to Ken, and if it was a girl, it stayed with the mom. Ken's kids were two and a half years apart and he had pulled his sperm back, so that he couldn't have any more right now.

Ken was a nice man. He was an electrician and worked with his hands a lot, which was a big bonus for me. I wanted to be worked over by those two big rough hands tonight. I felt the fire ignite in my crotch as I looked at his hands and big thick fingers. Ken was equally as curious about my time in Service and the day that my mark appeared. I'm sure he was a little worried that one of his sons would become marked on their thirteenth birthday, like I was.

I answered all of his questions and assured him that I had the opportunity of a lifetime and that I would not change a thing about it, including not being marked. He said he could tell that I had a lot of money and he was most shocked by my confidence and character. I think I was breaking all of his stereotypes about marked men.

I had repeatedly ignored the stares of the other patrons in the restaurant, as well as the waiter. I knew that most of them assumed that Ken was my Master and that I was in Service. Let them. I paid the bill, despite Ken's protests, and we headed for the car.

"Ken, do you mind if I drive around Calabash and Little River a little to see what has changed?"

"Not at all." He almost looked relieved.

We drove around and I told him where things used to be and how I saw that they had changed, and before I knew it, we were headed back to my house. Ken was properly impressed, even though he couldn't see the views. I got us both a dark rum on ice and took it out to the porch. He followed. We sat down in the rocking chairs and sipped our drinks.

"How old are you, Ken?"

He hesitated, which in my book, usually meant shame. "I'm thirty-four."

"And you're ashamed of that?" I asked, curious.

"No, but I can tell you are a lot younger than me."

"I'm twenty-four," I said, flatly.

"Oh, you look younger than that."

I laughed. "Thanks!"

"I'm just not sure why you would want to be—with me," he blurted out.

"I like you as a person and I'm sexually attracted to you. Those are my only two criteria."

He relaxed and blew a breath out. "Well, cheers to that!" We clinked our glasses together. "I think you are pretty hot."

"Thanks again, Ken. You know that you don't have to butter me up. I'm a done deal," I said as I finished my drink. "Shall we go?" I didn't wait for the answer, already knowing it.

I walked inside, telling him to lock the doors behind him. Putting more ice in our glasses, I felt the coolness of the marble countertops and had an idea. I poured more rum in the glasses and then moved forward into Ken's personal space, causing him to back up against the island.

Slowly, I begun to unbutton his shirt. Once it was open, I ran my hand over his chest. It was thick, strong, and covered in light blond hair. I looked into his eyes and I wasn't sure what I saw—maybe fear, but definitely lust. I dropped to my knees, keeping my hand on his chest. Using the other hand, I unbuttoned his shorts and let them drop. He was wearing boxer-briefs, which I pulled down swiftly with a yank on the waistband.

As if by itself, Ken's cock popped out of his underwear and bounced in front of my face. It was thick but average in length, protruding out of a thicket of blond pubic hair. I grabbed it around the shaft and held it up for my inspection. Flicking my tongue at the pee-hole, I captured his first drop of pre-cum and swallowed it down. It was delicious. As I looked up at him I said, "Very nice cock, Ken." He was staring down at me, looking like he was going to pass out. "You okay?" I asked him.

"Yeah. Better than okay. This is so fucking surreal!"

"*Don't* use that word. It's one of my pet peeves," I said, disgusted.

"Sorry. They do overuse it on reality shows all the time."

"People everywhere use it constantly," I said, before I put his soft cock head into my mouth and sucked on it. He rewarded me with more pre-cum and I released my hold on his shaft so I could engulf his entire cock into my mouth. Ken moaned with pleasure and put his hands on the back of my head, holding me on his cock. My nose was buried in that golden nest of hair and I could smell his intoxicating man-scent.

I started to work him over, pistoning up and down on that fat cock, and Ken responded by getting hard fast. I wasn't sure how his stamina was, being older, so I decided to not blow him all the way but get right to the fucking. I stood up, grabbed the bottle of lube from the great room, and asked Ken if he was ready. He nodded his head as his gaze followed my ass.

I came back in front of him and stripped off my clothes. Squirting lube on my palm, I greased up his fat monster. Hopping onto the marble countertop, I propped my back against the low-hanging cabinets. I placed each of my feet flat on the countertop outside my hips so that I was completely open to him. Holding up the lube bottle, I shook it, and he came over and held out that big hand that had turned me on so much. The lube flowed easily onto his big fingers and I smiled to let him know that it was okay to proceed.

"I love those big rough fingers inside me." I moaned.

I was sure Ken had never finger-fucked anyone before, but he turned out to be a world-class champion. His big, thick, rough fingers were perfect for the task and I was soon sweating and moaning under his sweet ministrations. He had both fingers in me and was muttering to himself about how tight I was.

"Fuck me, Ken." I finally groaned. He looked up at me, breaking the spell he was under playing with my ass. He smiled and pulled his fingers out, wiping them on a towel on the counter beside me. Ken replaced his fingers with his cock, pointing the head at my little hole and pushing forward with his hips.

I held myself in place by grabbing the edge of the countertop, not letting myself slide back any as he pushed inside me. My anal ring spread wide to let him in, which sent waves of purple pleasure straight from my ass to my brain and then to my own cock. Ken kept pushing until he was completely buried inside me, and then he looked up at me with a look of wonder on his face.

"Fuck! This is the most fantastic thing I have ever felt," he said, sounding slightly breathy. He held it there.

"You've fucked before," I said, almost too quickly.

"Yeah, at a Service Station. But this is something entirely different. And your ass is unbelievable."

"Your cock is pretty fantastic also," I told him. "Now, fuck me, Ken."

Ken didn't hesitate. He proceeded to send that fat monster down my anal chamber over and over. He was obsessed with watching it plunge inside my tight hole and again as he pulled it back out. Ken seemed to be unable to keep the pace while he was so excited, because he soon buried himself to the hilt in me and exploded with his release. His load was large and hot and I milked him with my ass muscles.

"Fuck me," Ken said hoarsely, his voice shaded with his need.

"That was a hot fuck, even though this marble is cold," I told him.

Ken pulled back and his cock popped out of me. I slid down off the counter and took his hand. Grabbing our glasses, I pulled him upstairs to the bed. Ken was able to rally and fuck me one more time before we showered and I drove him home.

"Have a great rest of the week with your kids, Ken," I said as I pulled up to the Mar Vista.

"Will I not see you again?"

"Probably on the beach. I would be more than happy to join you and the kids there." I made my message very clear, the way Patrick had taught me.

"Thanks, Brand . . . for everything."

"Thank you, Ken." And with that he was gone.

CHAPTER FOUR

My relaxing vacation was turning out to be just that. I was feeling more and more carefree as the days went by. Watching the ocean while I ate a toasted bagel, I planned out my day. I realized as I looked at the dazzling sun on the water that I was used to being with someone, and I wanted that for myself again. Having only been away from Patrick for a few days, I knew that I wanted to be with someone and share my life with them. I felt a relief knowing that I had come to this conclusion so quickly in my vacation, but I knew I had quite a bit of soul searching to do before I was truly on my chosen path.

Packing my cooler for the beach, I headed out. I had decided to stay at my beach today, to avoid any uncomfortable interactions with Ken, or with Brock, for that matter. There were a few people out and a lot of people were walking up and down the beach, either going to the pier or collecting shells, which I had noticed were more numerous on this strand of the beach.

I set up camp and went to ride the waves. The sea was rough and the undercurrent particularly strong. I enjoyed being one of the few people in the water and rode multiple waves before realizing that I had travelled down the beach quite a way. I decided to just keep riding and walk back up the beach when I was finished.

I rode one huge wave, catching it at just the right time and riding it almost to the shore. I was so excited when I bounded back out to the waves, hoping to catch another one exactly the same way. The next one I took didn't have the same power and I only went ten feet or so. When I stood up out of the water, wiping the saltwater off my face, he was right in front of me.

Startled, I said, "Hey."

It was my tan God from the inflatable boat. He was magnificently tall and handsome. I was six-foot-two, and he was at least two inches taller than me. His teeth were straight and white and his smile, while not large, was slightly crooked in a very sexy way.

"Not as good as your last one, but still not bad," he said with a broad grin as he caught the next wave and rode away from me. The bottoms of his feet were bright white compared to the golden tan of the rest of his body, and they were all I could see of him as he surfed away. He was older than I had originally thought, and I was surprised to see him alone, without his Servant. Turning my back to him, I waited for the next wave to catch, but didn't find it. There was a lull in the waves and I floated for a while before feeling his presence behind me.

Turning around, I looked him right in the face. He wore a kind expression, and I noticed that the parts of his face were all particularly average. There was nothing about his face that was exceptional except his amazing tan, but as a whole the average parts were quite nice together.

"You are pretty good at riding those waves, yourself," I said lamely.

"I'm pretty good at a lot of things." He smiled and said, "I'm Sam."

His statement floored me and I noticed right away that he was not nervous in front of me like most NOMARs. The pilot light in my balls immediately ignited. "Brand," I said back. "Where's your . . . um, friend, today?"

"My brother?"

His brother? "Is your brother marked?" I asked quickly.

He cracked a huge grin and said, "Yes."

Before I could say anything, Sam caught a huge wave that broke behind me and rode it into the shore. I caught the next one and noticed that Sam was walking out of the water and up to his towel. I didn't have any reason to follow him, so I walked back up the beach to my umbrella and chair, thinking about our encounter all the way.

By the time I got to my chair and sat down, I was as horny as I possibly could be. My encounter with Sam had taken its toll on me, both physically and mentally. I knew that I was drawn to him in some way that I couldn't explain. I also knew that I needed him to fuck me. The fact that his brother was marked explained why he was not nervous in front of me, and I was instantly attracted to him in so many ways.

I constantly scanned the beach for the sight of Sam, but never saw him again. He had quite a habit of disappearing on me.

And then some relief came into sight. A group of young studs were walking down the beach from the pier. There were at least seven of them, but one was clearly in charge. He was the shortest, but the most well-built. Sandy blond hair hung in his face and he had one of the cockiest walks I had ever seen. He was a cocky eighteen-year-old in his prime.

Cocky was scanning the beach as his band walked along. He saw me easily on the sparsely populated beach but didn't see my mark until he was much closer. As soon as he saw it, he looked from my jaw up to my eyes. I winked at him at that precise moment, and I saw him physically twitch like he had been stunned. He said something to his boys, and they kept walking while he stopped. He watched them go a few steps and then he turned towards me. He covered the distance between us in a few strides.

"Hey," he said, more cowed now than cocky.

"Hey."

"I'm Marco."

"Brand."

"So you're marked?" He was the master of the obvious.

"Yes, and you're not."

"No, I'm not," he said happily, while stroking his jaw line.

"How old are you, Marco?"

"Twenty one." I gave him a withering look. "Eighteen," he admitted. He flexed his biceps as if to make up for his young age.

I wasn't that impressed with him so far and decided to cut to the chase. "You wanna fuck, Marco?"

"Hell yeah!" he crowed while he grinned.

"You're very eager . . ." I was taught by Patrick to be very cautious of eagerness. "Would you want to go to dinner first?"

"Do I need to?"

"If you wanna fuck . . ."

"Okay," he conceded. He was going to have to win me over at dinner, because so far, I wasn't having it.

"Be in front of this house at six tonight," I told him as I pointed over my shoulder.

"All right."

"See you then, Marco."

"Okay." He headed after his boys, slowly at first and then much faster, breaking out in a full run.

My day certainly was anything but boring, that was for sure. I sat drinking and people watching for quite some time after that. When I finally felt like maybe I was getting too much sun, I gathered my things and headed inside the house. I took a quick shower and got dressed in cargo shorts, t-shirt, and flip-flops.

Marco was on time, driving up at a few minutes before six. He wanted to drive, so I let him. We decided on Mexican and headed to El Burro Loco in Myrtle Beach. I wasn't quite ready for the show that Marco put on once we got there, but put one on, he did. His cocky walk was back and even more exaggerated, I saw as we left the car and headed inside.

I put my name in with the host and noticed that Marco was watching the looks we were getting, even more closely than I was. He seemed to enjoy the attention and puffed out his chest in response. We only had to wait a few minutes and Marco used that time to put on as many airs as he could.

"Fancy yourself my Master?" I asked him, a little disgusted.

"That would be so gangster, wouldn't it?" His eyes were alight with excitement.

"You have to earn it, not just luck into it." I was still staring at him when the host came and escorted us to a booth. We sat, and Marco continued to posture to the tables around us. Thank God the big table right beside us was empty. I saw him make a smiling nod to a passing waiter, rubbing his jaw line to draw attention to mine.

"Marco, don't be an asshole," I said to him in a stern tone.

"Just having a little fun," he said sheepishly.

"Don't do it again," I warned.

He looked at me strangely, my guess was to see if he could test me or not. The waiter came over to take our orders.

"Go ahead," I told Marco.

"I'll have the beef fajita special and my Servant, uh, I mean my friend will have the enchiladas."

The waiter's eyes got big and he stared at me. I was furious with Marco. I turned toward the waiter and said, "He'll have his to go. Thank you."

The waiter left and I turned on Marco. "We're done. There's no way in hell I'm going to fuck with you when I don't even like you. Take your food and go home."

He sputtered, "But-but-I was—"

"Stop sniveling and go. You're making a fool out of yourself." I used the commanding voice and body posture that Patrick and my professors at The Service Academy had taught me.

Marco finally looked ashamed. "But I have the car."

"I'll get a cab."

"Are you sure? If I'm good, can we—"

Cutting him off with no hope, I said, "I'm sure."

Marco hung his head and got up from the booth. He left without looking back, his stride considerably more humble. When I turned back to the table, I realized that the big table beside me had been filled with people during our little drama. It was a family, judging by the slight resemblance amongst them. It was a father in his 50's and four brothers each in their late 20's and early 30's. There were three little boys under the age of five. And they were all looking at me.

"I'm sorry if that was a bother," I said to them.

The father, the obvious head of this family, said, "No problem, he sounded like an asshole. Are you okay?"

"Yes, sir. Thank you."

What looked like the oldest son said, "We were ready to take him out for you." This got a laugh from everyone. "But you certainly can take care of yourself."

"I can," I agreed as my food came. I started to eat and then I noticed how hot the men in this family were.

The father was bald, not so great-looking, but with incredible big biceps that wouldn't even fit in his shirt sleeves. The oldest son had dark hair cut short and a soul patch on his heavily shadowed face. He was good-looking and had nice biceps that were not as big as his dad's, but very nice. The next brother had a full black beard and shaggy hair. The third brother had a shaved head and a clean face. The fourth and the youngest son had his dark hair pulled back in a ponytail and the makings of the fantastic body that must have run in his family.

The food was good, and my protectors cut their eyes at me throughout the meal. As I finished the enchilada plate, I decided to try to turn my bad luck with Marco to my favor. I threw down more than enough cash to pay for my meal and Marco's. Standing up, I walked over to the family's table and put my card down on the table in front of the father.

"I'm grateful that your family was there for me tonight. I'm Brand, and I would love to reward you guys tomorrow night, if you want."

"Really?" the older son asked in shock.

"Yes," I said with a smile.

"Hot damn," the dad said, laughing. He held out his hand to me and I shook it. "We're the Janowicz's. Nice to meet you, Brand."

"You, too."

He turned to his boys and said, "Well, what about it fellas? Do we want to take Brand up on his offer?"

"Yes."

"Absolutely."

"We'll need to find some childcare."

"Yes." They were all in agreement.

"Maybe I can come to your place tomorrow after the kids have gone to bed," I offered. Patrick had always warned me against such actions, but I figured since they were small kids, that nothing bad could happen.

"Sure, that works," the father said.

"We'll text you the address," the older son said, looking at my card.

Smiling, I said, "See you tomorrow night, then." I left the restaurant, asking the host to call a cab for me before going out into the night air. My night hadn't been a total waste after all. The trip home was quick, and I fell into the big bed, exhausted, and fell right to sleep.

I woke up in a good mood and wondered if I would see Sam today. Having to rest up for the Janowicz's tonight, I told myself that I shouldn't go to the beach today, but I did want to see Sam, if possible. So I decided to just take a walk on the beach and see if I ran into him.

Walking down the beach, I spotted him in the water before I even got to him. Sam was like a god in the surf, and I was transfixed by the sight of him. His physical presence drew me to him more than anyone else I had ever met before. He was jumping waves, and he was alone. I headed into the water at an angle that would allow me to get to him quicker.

Sam saw me coming, smiled, and waved to me. I joined him shortly and found myself suddenly shy. "Hi, Sam."

"Hey." He regarded me with interest. Sam's golden eyes glittered in the bright sunlight. "Michael has a ton of questions he would like me to ask you."

"Michael is your brother?"

"Yes."

"I would like to talk with him."

Sam hesitated, and I thought I saw the shadow of a distant thought cross his handsome face. "I'm not sure me or my father would like you to . . ."

This hit me like a blow. "Why not?"

"He's only fourteen. There are probably a lot of things that he shouldn't know yet."

"Isn't he going to one of The Service Academies?"

"Probably."

"Then he will know all in just a little while."

Sam looked defeated. "We just want to keep him a kid as long as we can."

I decided to change tactics and not be so in his face. "I respect that. Maybe I could answer some of his questions with you and your dad present."

Relief crossed Sam's face, and I instantly was happy with myself for being the one that provided him with that calming quality. "That might be a good idea. I will ask dad and let you know."

"Cool." I wanted to take my standard direct approach and ask him to go fuck, but I was afraid of scaring him off. I decided to take a more tactful approach. "Sam, I'd like it if you came to my house this afternoon." I felt the draw of my body to his like we were magnetic.

"You would?" he teased me, obviously knowing what I was asking for, but not playing along.

"I would, smart ass," I said, poking his shoulder with a finger. "It's the grey one right over there."

Sam followed my finger with his gaze as I pointed towards my house. "In the ritzy section?" He smirked.

"Yeah." I couldn't take my gaze off his.

"I'll think about it." I could see the shadow cross his face again.

I could tell Sam was conflicted, but I wasn't sure why, unless he just wasn't into me. But I swear I could feel the sexual tension between us. It was telling to me that he didn't ask what I wanted with him. He knew, just like I did. "Okay. Well, I'll be there, if you want to come."

"Okay." Sam's eyes never left mine.

Trying to leave while feeling that magnetic pull between us was one of the hardest thing I have ever had to do. "See ya later." I tried to sound nonchalant, but I think I came off as a little desperate. I turned and made my way through the water and back to the beach. I wanted to turn around and continue to look at Sam, but I wouldn't let myself.

It was a stunning day to be at the beach, and I sat on the porch and waited for Sam, trying to read a book. I drank a beer to try to relax, but it didn't seem to help much. The wait was nerve-wracking and tedious. There weren't many people to look at on the beach and I couldn't concentrate enough to read. After several hours, I gave up on Sam coming over and went to take a nap. My sleep was disturbed by dreams of a giant golden dolphin coming at me through the waves, but when I tried to reach out and touch it, it would just swim away.

CHAPTER FIVE

When I woke up, I couldn't help but be disappointed that Sam had not visited. I told myself that he probably had a good reason and I set about getting ready for tonight. I fixed spaghetti with a meat sauce for my dinner and watched the TV shows that I had recorded last night.

Before I knew it, the time had flown by and I needed to go meet the Janowzicz's. I put a bottle of lube in my pocket and went down to my car. The night was really humid, and I felt myself sweating just walking down to the car. I drove to the address that they had texted me with the air conditioning blasting and found them to be staying in a single family house on stilts, just like the one my family used to stay in when we came to the beach all those years ago.

I walked up the stairs, up to the screened porch and knocked softly on the door, remembering that the kids were supposed to be asleep. One of the brothers opened it for me and let me in. Everyone greeted me warmly, and the father handed me a beer.

"The kids asleep?" I asked, noticing that they were watching the NBA Finals on TV.

"In the back room," the father said.

"So, whose who here?" I asked, looking at the assembled men.

"I'm Jim," the dad said. "Jake's my oldest." Jake was the one with the shaved head and soul patch. "Then John." He had the beard. "And then came Joe." Joe was the shaved head with no facial hair. "And then we got Julian." The youngest one who had the ponytail.

"Nice to meet everyone. J names, huh?"

"Just for you, Brand," Julian tossed out.

"The kids are in the back bedroom, so we thought maybe we could just use this front bedroom and we would just go in one at a time," Jim told me.

"One at a time? I thought we would just let it be organic and see what happens."

"Nah. We just thought you would be more comfortable with us one at a time," Jim said.

"I appreciate that, but I kinda like the group dynamic sometimes," I told him as I took another swig of beer. "So, who's the best fuck out of you and your boys, Jim?"

He immediately answered me. "I am, of course."

The boys all laughed. Jake said, "I remember the first time he took me to a Service Station and tried to show me how to do it."

"Jesus, Jake whacked off so much that he wouldn't let me have a moment's peace," Jim said, laughing.

"And none of your boys came out with the mark, Jim?"

"Not a one. But they all are the best fuckers you've ever seen," he said, his voice full of pride.

"I'll be the judge of that," I smirked as I pulled the bottle of lube out of my pocket and put it on the side table.

"Cheers to that," Joe said, holding up his beer. We copied him and toasted to it as well.

"Well let's get to it," I said, not willing to continue the banter anymore. I stood up and stripped off my clothes, giving them a show, especially of my behind.

The boys responded by standing up and undressing as well. Joe and John were the closest ones to me, so I dropped to my knees in front of them. Their cocks were thick but average in length. They each fed them to me as I knelt and I hungrily sucked them in. Their cocks were salty and musky.

I took turns sucking them until I spun around and sucked two more. Looking up, I saw that they belonged to Julian and Jake. Jake's cock was long and thick, where Julian's appeared long and skinny. I worked one with each hand while I sucked on one.

Reaching out to the next one, I got a huge surprise. Jim's cock was really long and really thick. I sucked around the circle, giving hand jobs more than blowjobs.

Coming off of Jim's big beast, I said, "I see who has the biggest wang in the group."

"It's gonna take a lot of lube." Jim smirked.

Jake sat down on the sofa and pulled me onto his lap facing away from him. He put his legs between mine, separating them. I felt his fingers on my puckered hole and heard the squirt of the lube bottle. The cold lube ran down my ass crack and he massaged it into my hole with one very large, very rough finger. From this vantage point, I could see all of the guys, except Jake, of course. Although they were all built fantastically, they all had different patterns of hair on their chest. Joe had a full chest of brown hair that also covered his belly. John had a treasure trail only. Jake and Jim both had umbrellas of hair that covered their pecs and went into a treasure trail. Julian was completely shaved clean.

John stepped up with Joe in front of me, and I bent to continue to suck their cocks while Jake lowered me down onto his fat slickened cock. He penetrated, stretching my anal ring around his thick girth as Jake lowered me further down onto his cock. It made me pause as I sucked on his brother's mighty tool.

"Fuck, he's tight." Jake groaned.

Jake set a good pace, moving his crotch up and down under me, sending his big cock into my hole and back out again, repeatedly. Jake's fucking of me also kept my mouth steady so that I could take turns blowing his father and brothers. I could feel Jake's cock expand in my ass as he reached his climax and I used my ass muscles to milk him dry after he exploded inside me.

I felt Jake's hands lifting my ass and I realized he wanted me to move. I straightened up and saw that John was sitting on the couch beside Jake now, holding up his stiff cock. I turned to face him and impaled myself on his big Johnson in one quick move. Jake's cum served as a nice lubricant.

"Fuck! That feels good," John said.

I enjoyed the feel of his beard scratching my chest as I begun to move up and down on him. Jim came around to the back of the couch and held out his big cock. I sucked it into my mouth and let my movements stroke him, even as I was stroking his son.

John grabbed my ass cheeks and held me still as he started to fucking tear me up from below. Jim was right—his boys certainly knew how to fuck. I looked behind me while sucking on the side of Jim's cock and saw that the other boys were stroking their big cocks as they waited their turns. This family was certainly right up my alley.

"I'm coming in this tight hole," John gasped as he pulled his cock out of me and shot strands of ropy hot cum onto my back and ass cheeks. Jim used a towel to wipe my back as John re-inserted his cock into my hole and milked more cum out of it.

"Joe, you're up," John called to him, but quietly.

"Let's go to the bed," Joe said as he headed to the door. Once there, I saw that the family had pushed together two full-size beds to form one giant one. Joe positioned me on my back with my head falling over one of the sides. Joe lifted my legs into the air and found my sweet spot.

I moaned as he pushed into me with his thick cock, stretching my anal ring wide. Joe was in his element and he proceeded to put on a grand performance. He bent me in half and leaned over me on thick arms, plowing a furrow into my anal channel. Julian walked over towards my head and pushed his cock into my mouth. I tried to give him good head, but it was difficult while I was being rocked by his brother.

Julian didn't seem to care how good I was at sucking cock because he used my open mouth to just be a hole for his face-fuck. Between Julian's big cock fucking into my mouth and his brother's fucking into my ass, I had rarely been spit-roasted so well.

"Fuck." Joe growled as he pulled his cock out of me and sprayed a load of hot semen on my stomach and balls. He traded places with Julian, and I sucked his cum off of his cock as he fed it into my mouth.

Julian wrapped my legs around his hips and slid his cock into my sore hole. He had a different style of fucking, preferring to undulate his hips in a wave motion that drove his skinny cock into my hole deeper and then back out again. His cock never really even left my ass more than half-way, but it felt like he was driving into me like a fucking piston.

Joe's cock softened in my mouth, so he let his dad take his place. Jim's cock was amazingly big with thick veins that stood out from the skin of his shaft. My lips stretched wide to accommodate his big girth. Julian's earthworm fuck was driving me insane and I fantasized about Jim's big cock pounding me hard. I decided to use my ass muscles to squeeze Julian's cock so that he would reach his climax faster—and I would get to Jim.

Much as I suspected, my ass muscles milked Julian's cock, causing him to bust his nut quicker than he planned, and he shot his hot load right in my ass.

"That's a pretty nice ass," Julian said as he slapped my cheeks and pulled out of me.

I returned the compliment as I stroked Jim's cock with my hand. "Thanks, Julian. Your fuck was pretty hot."

"All right, if you guys are finished blowing smoke up each other's asses, I want to fuck you," Jim said.

I was soon on all fours on top of the bed. Julian fed his cock to me and it tasted like cum from all of his brothers. I sucked him down while Jim inserted three fingers into my ass and stretched it out. I moaned in response, felt his big cockhead resting on my puckered hole, and then felt the pain as he slammed his cock into me.

Red fingers of pain shot up my spine and rushed to my brain. Jim held it there, letting me get used to it. The red pain soon turned to purple pleasure spikes radiating from his giant cock in my ass.

"Wow! Brand, you just serviced my four sons and you're still as tight as you can be. Impressive."

I took Julian's cock out of my mouth and said, "Thanks, Jim. Now shut up and tear that thing up!"

Jim accepted my challenge and fucking ripped me a new one. He set a furious pace and I wondered how long he could keep it up since he had been waiting so long. But he was definitely impressing me as he fucked like he was a magician, sawing me in half with his huge saw. The rest of the poor family had to endure my grunts and moans as a result of the strain of their father's thrusts.

"You ready for me to plant my seed in you?" Jim asked.

"Plant a whole fucking garden," I told him, not wanting him to stop fucking me with that long fat cock.

Jim fucked me right through his climax. He shot hot strands of cum deep into my ass as he continued to pound that cock into me and pull it back out. It was a hot fuck and impressive for a guy of his age. I guess I had some things to learn about stereotypes myself.

"Fuck! That's a nice piece of ass," Jim said, to the room as much as to me.

The six of us spent the next hour enjoying each other's

special skills. I think by the end of the night, I had been fucked eight times.

"Mind if I shower before I go?" I asked Jim.

"Feel free, man. You've earned it."

"I feel like I'm a freaking cum bucket. You guys are beasts!" I said with a laugh. "I guess I'm just lucky that the kids aren't old enough to fuck yet, or I'd be dead right about now."

"You not used to getting that much cock on a daily basis?" Joe asked me.

"No. My Master preferred more of a one-to-one arrangement."

"But you have fucked multiples before, right?" Jake asked. "I mean, you seemed really comfortable."

"Oh, yeah. For sure. I'm just a little out of practice."

"We couldn't tell. You did yourself proud, Brand, and we appreciate it," Jim said with sincerity.

"Thanks, guys." I headed to the shower and used the shower wand to try to spray some of that cum out of my ass before I made my way home. My legs felt like butter and my ass was radiating a good burn as I dried off and redressed in the main room.

There was a chorus of thanks from the guys. I told them what a good time I had as I said my good-byes.

I headed home and slipped into a coma-like sleep on top of the bed when I got there.

CHAPTER SIX

The next day was another beautiful day at the beach, so I decided to start it at the pool before going out to the beach. I packed my stuff in the car and headed out. The Waipani pool was comforting to me in its sameness. The C shape with the giant palm tree in the middle reminded me of fond times from before I went into The Service.

I had the pool to myself, so I threw my towel down on a lounger and dived in. The water was cool, and I enjoyed swimming the length of the pool underwater, opening my eyes as I did. The way the bright sunshine was being filtered through the clear water was beautiful to me and I couldn't get enough of it. I finally came up at the ladder of the shallow end and saw that I wasn't alone anymore. A couple of dads had set up camp with their kids in tow.

One of the dads was cute, bald and buff. Based on his body shape, I guessed he was probably a runner. His cock made a substantial bulge in his bathing suit as he walked down the stairs into the water, holding his son's hand. I guessed he was in his late twenties, but the bald head might have thrown me off.

Bald dad was really good with his kid, and I liked him all the better for it. I smiled at them and headed up the ladder to my lounge chair. I saw the bald dad do a double-take when he noticed the mark. The double take was subtle, but there, and I smiled to myself as I stretched out in the sun right beside the lip of the pool.

The sun was hot and I was just contemplating whether to

get back into the pool or go down to the beach when I heard a small voice near me. I pulled my baseball hat off my face and looked down to see the bald dad's kid in a float, looking up at me.

"Hi," he said, waving his chubby hand at me.

"Hi. What's your name?"

The bald dad intervened. "Tell him, *my name is Riley*."

"Hi, Riley." Riley suddenly lost interest in me and held his hands out for his dad. "How old is he?"

"He's two. I'm Raif, by the way," he said with a significant accent.

"Raif, I'm Brand. Are you German?"

"Yeah."

"I love the accent. My family is German, as well."

"Where from?"

I chuckled and answered, "We are American. We came over so long ago, nobody remembers."

"Oh yeah? You enjoying your vacation?"

"So far so good. I just finished six years in The Service and now I'm enjoying some of the money I earned."

"Really? I mean I noticed the mark, but I didn't know."

"Yeah. Just finished on Friday."

"Wow! You did just finish."

I nodded and stayed silent.

Riley cooed as he spun in the water. Raif looked at me a little nervously and blurted out, "Man, I know this is kinda crazy since we just met, but I was wondering if you would like to watch the Finals with me tonight."

It *was* sudden and crazy, and I was taken aback by it.

He continued, hoping to make his case. "I've been down here with Riley all by myself, and I'm yearning for some adult stimulation, so to speak."

I laughed at that.

"And every night, once I put him down, I am kinda stuck

there, unable to leave or do anything." He let a big breath as he finished.

I smiled at him and said, "I can understand. Why don't you and Riley come over to my house and you can put him down in one of the spare bedrooms and sleep over."

I saw from his face that he was stunned by this proposition and didn't quite know what to say.

"My TV is larger," I said as explanation.

"I don't know. The one in the place I'm renting here is a fifty-two inch."

"I've got an eighty-four inch monster . . . TV that is . . ." I laughed out loud at my joke.

"Wow and wow," he said, starting to laugh, too. Riley also joined us, laughing and clapping his fat hands.

"All right," he finally said, smiling.

I gave him a card, told him to text me, and let him know that I would text him my address back. We said our goodbyes and I headed down to the beach.

Hopeful to see Sam, I walked down the beach access and picked a spot. I didn't see Sam and I was still a little disappointed with him that he hadn't come by yesterday afternoon, so I lied to myself that I was okay with not getting to see him today. Once my umbrella and chair were up, I headed down to the water. I swam and body surfed for quite a while before getting out and re-applying sunscreen.

Still no sign of Sam! I moved my chair down to the water's edge and pulled a magazine out of the back of my chair. I loved sitting in the water, reading, and watching the guys walk by. I did see Ken playing with his boys in the surf and waved to him. He waved back and looked like he wanted to come over, but thought better of it.

Suddenly, my chair jerked backwards like I was going to collapse, but after I jerked myself upright, I realized it was someone behind me. I could feel his presence before I turned my head and confirmed that it was Sam.

"Hey. What are you doing on the poor man's beach?" he asked with a smirk, stepping around beside me.

"It's where you are," I said flatly.

He looked shameful and hung his head. "Hey, sorry I didn't come yesterday. Dad, Michael, and I went to play par three golf, and it took longer than I thought it would."

"No problem," I said coolly.

He sat down beside me on the sand, "You wanna do something tonight . . . watch TV or something?"

I looked at him as if I could tell whether he would show up or not simply by looking at his face. "I can't . . . already got plans." I enjoyed seeing the look on his face after I said it.

"Really? What?"

Before I could answer, Michael bounded down in front of us. His face lit up when he saw who Sam was talking to.

I stood up and held out my hand, "You must be Michael."

"Yes. Are you Brand?"

"Yes."

I could see the teenager checking out my mark, even as I was doing the same thing to him. "Sam and dad have been talking about you."

"They have?" I made my voice sound mockingly surprised.

"Yes, we have," Sam answered. "Dad and I would like you to be able to talk with Michael . . . with us," he said nervously.

Watching the waves crest high, Michael turned to us and pleaded, "Let's go in the water."

"Okay," Sam said. "Brand, you wanna come?"

"Sure," I said, standing up and moving my chair back up to my umbrella. I followed Sam and Michael into the deep water and started riding over the waves with them. It was fun to get to know them better and to see their interaction with each other. They were brothers, prone to fight and disagree, but they cared for each other a lot. It was good to see and told me a lot about Sam as a person.

We had a lot of fun and started to ride the waves into the shore. I loved playing with them, and I was able to jump on Sam's broad back several times, which was so fucking hot to me. Michael seemed to be very comfortable with me, and I liked him as a person, as well.

"Well, guys, I'm starving so I'm going to head back in," I said to them.

"Ask him, Sam," Michael whined.

I turned expectantly to Sam, studying his face. I was so horny for him that my head was swimming just looking into his handsome mug.

"We would like you to go out to dinner with us tomorrow night, if you're free," Sam said, adding the last bit with a sarcastic tone.

"For sure!" I said excitedly.

"Awesome," Michael said.

"Awesome," Sam repeated.

"Awesome," I repeated, before heading into the shore. Walking up to my chair and drying off, I sat down, opened a beer, and ate a sandwich. I had lost track of Sam and Michael in the water, but I had a great overall feeling for today as far as they were concerned.

A little while later, Sam appeared under my umbrella. I held a beer out to him and he took it, flashing me a brilliant smile as he sat down on the sand.

"Michael really likes you," he told me.

"I'm more interested in whether Michael's brother really likes me or not."

He bit his lower lip and hung his head. "Jesus, you're direct!"

"I don't like to waste time or energy."

Sam nodded and said, "I wanted to give you my cell phone

number so we could make plans for dinner tomorrow." He handed me a slip of paper with his digits on it.

"I liked Michael, as well."

"He's a good kid. Thanks for spending time with us today. I really enjoyed it."

"Me, too." I let the words just hang there, knowing not to talk too much.

Sam finished his beer, handed me the empty bottle, and stood up. He walked around me, slapping me on the shoulder with his big hand, before he leaned down to whisper in my ear, "Cancel your plans tonight."

"What?" I asked in shock, but he was gone.

I packed up all of my beach gear and drug it to the car. Driving back to the house, I tried to piece all of our conversations back together. Not even unloading the car, I went upstairs and showered. I jacked off in the shower, fantasizing about Sam and me rolling around in the surf and fucking. It temporarily eased the sexual tension in my body, but it didn't last.

Drying off, I phoned Raif and cancelled our date. If there was even a chance that Sam might come over tonight, I wanted to give him that chance. Raif was disappointed, but I left it open to do again, so that gave him a little hope. After I hung up, I lay down naked on the cool bed sheets and took a nap.

When I woke, it was getting dark. I threw on some basketball shorts and a t-shirt and set to making my house look lived-in. Even though Sam didn't say he was coming over, I was so excited about the possibility of it that my body practically rang with tension. The beach house soon looked great and I had set low mood lighting. I decided to wait on the porch and enjoy the ocean breeze.

Nightfall came quickly as I rocked on the porch. After an hour or so, I considered calling Sam, since I had his cell phone number now, but thought better of it. I was tired of giving him opportunities and him not taking them. It was getting to a point where I was starting to look desperate, and I didn't like that. In most of my interactions with men, I always had the upper hand, but I was feeling out-of-control with Sam and I didn't care for it at all.

My phone finally read ten o'clock, so I started to go inside, but then I saw movement at the porch door. I could feel that it was him. I had the door latched, so I walked over to it. It was Sam. I unlatched it without saying anything and sat back down. He came in, latched the door back, and sat down in the chair beside me.

"You mad at me?" he asked softly.

"Why would I be mad at you?"

"Because I asked you to cancel your plans and then I didn't come over."

"You are here, now."

"I've actually been here for a while . . . watching you," he said sheepishly.

"Why?" For the life of me, I couldn't figure this man out.

"I was glad to see that you cancelled your plans."

"I want to be with you, Sam." There. I said it, as plainly as I could say it.

"I know you do."

"But?"

"I don't know if I—"

"If you want to be with me?"

"No, if I *should* be with you. I want to be."

This hit me like a ton of bricks. I had just assumed all this time that he wasn't interested, even though I thought I could read his body language. "What do you mean, whether you should?"

"My dad says it will be a mistake. That once a NOMAR has that type of connection with a marked guy, that they can't go back."

"Why would you want to go back, once you have that connection?" I challenged him, even though I knew he was probably right.

"And I'm not sure it is a good example for Michael."

This part I could understand. But at the same time, Michael seemed to like me, and if he saw two people that cared about each other together, wouldn't that be a good example?

"And it's illegal." He looked up into my eyes with a smirk on his face.

"A law that is rarely enforced if both parties are consenting."

"Of course, the only one that is important to me is what it might do to Michael."

"What if it is good for Michael?"

I could see in his eyes that he had never even considered this. The next part was hard for him, based on his nervousness and his body language. "I like the way I feel when I'm around you and I like you as a person. I'm a great judge of character, and I don't think I'm wrong about you."

"So . . ."

"So, I want to do the right thing."

"So, I'm the wrong thing?"

"No, not at all. Is that the way you feel?"

"A little . . . like I'm trying to convince you to do something bad."

"I'm pretty sure it would be something good," he said, laughing with his eyes, as well as his mouth.

I returned his lasciviousness, looking at him directly in the eyes. "I can guarantee you that it will be fantastic."

He swallowed hard. "I want to be good, but I'm weak. I wanted just to see if you were going to cancel your plans or not. I knew I should have left after that, but I couldn't. I could see you up here and I wanted to be with you and to . . ."

"To what?"

"To make you feel better."

I regarded him for a moment. "You make me feel good, and then bad, and then good again. It's like a relationship with someone who is abusive."

"Really?" He looked miserable. "I guess I've never seen it from your point of view before. I'm sorry. Really sorry." Very uncomfortable, he got up and headed for the door. "Text me tomorrow about dinner."

And then he was gone.

Chapter Seven

When Sam left me alone on the porch, I felt empty. And then I realized that I was *hungry* as well as upset. It was almost eleven, and I remembered that Georgio's on Main Street was still open so I called in a pizza order. It was time to eat away my feelings.

I jumped in the car and drove to the Dairy Hut off of Ocean Drive in Cherry Grove and got my favorite, a large chocolate soft-serve with wet walnuts. I drove back to the house, ran it up to the freezer, ran back down the stairs, and drove to Georgio's.

I was surprised that the older guy that always ran the pizza shop wasn't there, for the first time since I had been coming. I did recognize some of the workers, who were traditionally Russian in nationality. North Myrtle Beach had a very successful exchange program for young Russians to come over to the US on work visas. I especially remembered the large one. He was about six-foot-six, long blond hair pulled back in a ponytail, and a thick body under his shirt.

Walking up to the part of the counter where I would pay, he greeted me. "Can I help you?" His English was far improved in the six years that I had been gone. His eyes quickly flicked to my mark and then back to my eyes with no change in his face.

"Pick-up for Brand."

He nodded and then went to check on the order. "Just a minute more." He found the order ticket and rang me up.

"Fourteen fifty-four."

I handed him the cash and was delighted to see that his hand was huge when he held it out. The fingers were well-formed and thick with well-manicured nails. I thought my hands were big, but they were like a child's compared to his. I must have paused a little too long, because when I looked up from his hand to his eyes, he was smiling.

"I have seen you before, no?"

"I used to come here every year, but I have been away for six years. I remember you from before," I said coyly.

"Yes, I thought so. Never forget a nice face."

Normally, I would not be this blunt or forward, but my meeting with Sam had left me feeling weird, and I was still hornier than hell. "Are you interested in seeing more?"

He stopped short and looked up at me with that poker face. "Yes, of course."

"What time do you get off work?"

"One."

"I'll be back to pick you up. What's your name?"

"Petor."

Just then my name was called further down the counter, so I said, "See you later, Petor."

He waved as I picked up my pizza and headed home. I was thrilled to have a liaison planned to take my mind off Sam, and I couldn't stop smiling from the excitement of the flirt, which was one of my favorite parts of a conquest.

The pizza was just as great as I remembered it and the ice cream was even better. I only made a dent in both of them and wrapped up the left-overs for another day. I only had to watch late-night TV for a little while before it was time to go pick up Petor. I almost ran down the stairs and had to tell myself to go the speed limit down Ocean Boulevard or I would get a ticket.

Petor was waiting outside the front of the pizza shop when I got there, even though I was early.

"Nice ride," he said in heavily accented English.

"Thanks. You ready to go?"

"Absolutely." Petor climbed into the car as I heard a bunch of muted cheers coming from the shop windows. Petor's Russian co-workers were pressed against the glass windows, whooping and cheering for him.

I smiled and Petor shrugged his shoulders. I drove off towards the house.

"Where have you been for six years?" Petor asked, showing me he was a good listener.

"I was in The Service."

"Oh, for six years?" He sounded incredulous.

"Yeah. I guess he liked me . . ." I let it hang out there suggestively.

"I guess, but he had to pay, yes?"

"Yes," I said, smiling and nodding my head. We pulled into the driveway, and his eyes lit up at the size of the house. It was the most expressive I had seen him.

"He paid, alright," Petor mumbled.

He made me laugh again. More pressing on my mind was how to get him in the shower. He smelled like a big pizza. The beach house probably did also, since that was what I'd had for dinner, but I wasn't going to be licking the house.

I unlocked the door and we went inside. He was very interested in looking around, so I let him while I got us drinks.

"Beer?" I held one up to him. He turned his nose up at it. "I don't have any vodka," I said, sarcastically.

He turned. "Not all Russians drink vodka." He paused. "Okay, I lie, we all do. But I really like rum also." He pointed at the bottle of dark brown gold on my counter.

"Rum it is," I said, as I poured us two glasses with ice. "You wanna shower?"

"Don't like me smelling like a pepperoni?"

Laughing, I said, "Want to suck your pepperoni, not smell

it. I'll shower with you."

He smiled and we headed upstairs where he continued to look around, amazed at the views and furnishings. We ended up in the master bathroom, and I undressed him as he stood still on the tile floor. Petor had an amazing chest, broad and muscular, but he had a thickness to the muscles instead of a cut. He had a slight belly and long legs held up by big feet. His cock was long with a thickness at the base and a tapered shaft.

When I had his shoes off and he was completely naked, I stripped for him. His gaze never left me as I turned and showed him my moneymaker while I was leaning into the glass shower, turning on the water. I saw him lick his lips when I turned back around. I stepped into the tiled shower and held the glass door for him. His cock pointed the way.

"I can't believe my good luck," he said as he ran his hand down my side and onto my ass cheeks.

"I think we are both lucky tonight," I told him as I soaped up a pouf and started to scrub him down, and then myself. His skin was unusually white for someone that lived at the beach, but I felt his power, like showering with a polar bear. After scrubbing his chest, stomach, and back, I dropped to my knees and cleaned his legs and feet before concentrating on his crotch.

I scrubbed his pubic hair, which was nicely trimmed, and then his un-cut cock, before holding it up to his abs and cleaning his ball sack and then his grundle. Once I had him rinsed off, I sucked his long cock into my hot mouth, enjoying his clean taste and smell.

Petor moaned his approval of using my mouth to vacuum his cock, and I enjoyed his big hand on the back of my head, forcing me deeper onto his hard cock. I had to stretch my mouth wider and wider as I got closer to the base, but I was able to take him all in without gagging, which I thought was quite a feat.

Petor pulled the rubber band out of his hair and let his blond locks fall about his shoulders before he stuck his head under the shower head.

I pistoned up and down on Petor's cock, pushing the water back out of my mouth with each thrust forward. Petor groaned as he reached his climax and his big hand became more insistent on my head. He finally buried deep and busted his nut, squirting his sweet cream into the back of my throat. I swallowed his cum down as I continued to keep the pressure on his cock, using my tongue to press the vein on the bottom, milking more cum out of him.

Petor moaned, "Jesus Christ."

His cock now clean, I had an itch that needed to be scratched, and there was no reason to wait. I stood up and he turned me around, facing away from him as he inspected my ass. I assumed the position against the heavy glass walls of the shower, spreading my legs wide. In my mind, I could see his big hand on my ass cheeks and then his long rough fingers inspecting my hole.

"Lube's on the shelf," I said, my voice husky with lust.

I heard him squirt the lube on his hand and then jack his cock back up hard. Then I felt the cold lube on my ass, running down my crack and into my hole. He made sure it went into my hole by inserting one of his big fingers inside me.

"So tight," Petor said with excitement.

"Sit down on the bench," I commanded him. He followed my orders without question or hesitation.

I stood on the bench on either side of his legs, holding onto the towel bar. Squatting, I lowered myself down and held myself elevated over his lap until he placed his hard cock head on my puckered hole. I pushed down with my ass and felt his little cock head pop inside me. I savored the feeling of my anal ring stretching wider and wider as I continued to lower myself down on his pyramid-shaped cock. Petor was long enough to scratch my itch, and he punched my prostate as he snaked deeper into my anal channel.

Soon I was fully impaled on his big monster and he was smiling up at me like a fool.

"Feels good?" I asked him as I tried to get used to him inside me.

"Fucking fantastic." He grinned. He put his hands on my chest and then onto my sides. Petor lifted me up and then pulled me back down. I felt like a doll in his giant hands, riding up and down on his long dick. He seemed to enjoy watching and manipulating me as he fucked, like most NOMARs did when they had sex with a marked man instead of at a Service Station.

"You're fucking up into me so deep." I moaned to him as he increased his speed and was fucking tearing me up from below.

Almost as if he knew the filthy thoughts in my head, Petor put a big hand on my face, inserted his thumb into my mouth and wrapped the rest of his fingers over my face.

I greedily sucked on that thumb and felt my cock get hard at his unusual hand placement. I moaned around his thumb as he continued to move me up and down on his big cock. His cock twitched in my ass and I could hear his change in breathing, so I knew he was close to falling over the edge. Sure enough, Petor thrust into me at the same time that he pulled me completely down onto his lap and blew his big load inside me.

"Fuck!" he exclaimed, out of breath. "It is good to be in America, no?"

"That was hot," I said, reminding myself of a certain marked celebrity who said that phrase constantly. I turned the water off and stepped off of Petor and out of the shower.

Using a washcloth to clean my ass and his cock, I got us both clean before drying us with big fluffy towels.

"Is this what it feels like to be a Master?" he asked me.

"How would I know?" I asked.

"You had a Master, did you not?"

"I did."

"So, this is kinda like the life you had with him. An expensive house, nice things, sex whenever and as often as you want it, and someone to wait on you."

"I guess. Patrick and I were more of a partnership. There was not so much of me waiting on him hand and foot." Of course, I told myself, he'd had plenty of servants to wait on him for those things.

"I didn't mean to offend."

"You didn't. You want to go again?"

"Love to. You?"

"Sure." We crawled up on the bed and I got on my back. I really needed to be dominated by this big Russian-American. Petor seemed to sense what I needed and lifted my legs, putting the soles of my feet flat on his chest. His cock was hard again and he wasted no time before burying it up to the nuts inside me.

Petor towered over me on the bed, but when he leaned over me, I was in heaven. He propped himself up on his arms and bent me back onto myself—my breath caught in my throat and my heart seemed to beat out of my chest. He proceeded to drill me into the mattress. His stamina was impressive, not having missed a beat between his two climaxes and now going for a third.

Petor set a nice rhythm to his thrusts and I tried to arch my back and push my ass back towards him each time he pushed forward. His balls swung in a wide arc, slapping my lower back like a wrecking ball tearing down a building. I put my hands on his biceps and held on while he plowed into me over and over again.

In the middle of this fuck, Petor buried to the hilt inside me and held there. I was caught off-guard by this and was a little confused by it at first. He was looking down at me with that face that was unreadable, and I wondered what was on his mind. I really liked the way his hair fell down around his head as he towered over me.

"Really nice ass," he finally said.

"Really nice cock," I answered, matching his tone.

Petor smiled and then rose onto his feet, lifting me into the air. He proceeded to drill into me from above like an oil derrick—his long cock thrusting into me over and over as I balanced on my neck and upper back. He continued to fucking tear me up until he blew his third load in me and collapsed onto the bed beside me.

"God damn," I sighed, contented.

"That's what I'm talking about," he said, using a truly American phrase.

I looked at the clock and saw it was after three in the morning, so I said, "Wanna spend the night, Petor?"

"Can we fuck again in the morning?" he asked, raising an eyebrow.

"Absolutely," I answered as I climbed under the covers.

CHAPTER EIGHT

The next morning, I took care of Petor's morning wood before getting fucked by him once more. We both showered and I drove him to his car at the pizza shop. He thanked me and showed his maturity by knowing that there was no hope in asking for more.

I drove back home and ate leftover pizza for lunch. I lay on the bed and texted Sam, feeling a little guilty about my late-night escapade.

Hey, you up?

It's nearly one . . . aren't you?

Shit!

Yes, of course. I thought you might be napping

Good recovery, Brand.

Who can nap when my mind is full of you?

Holy Shit!

Well, that is good news for me!!!!

Dad wants to go to Calabash tonight. That okay with you?

Sure

Meet us here at Waipani C-20 at five-thirty. Need directions?

Hardly!

Nope, I got it! See u then

Yep

Well, this should be interesting.

Dinner was going to consist of two marked guys, one of whom wanted the dirt on The Service, but whose dad and brother didn't want him to hear it. The other one had a thing for the brother, who had admitted he was interested, but didn't want to act on it. Dinner should be a hot mess and very entertaining for those people eating around us. I was very titillated with the thought of Sam sitting around thinking of me and was overjoyed that he'd told me so.

It was late in the day already, so I decided not to go to the beach today. I stripped the bed and threw the sheets into the wash and left to do some shopping at the Tanger Outlets. I didn't see much that I had to have, so I wound up not buying anything.

Patrick called me while I was shopping and told me that he just got the results of our latest investments and that we had made a quarter of a million dollars profit. I couldn't even wrap my head around that and I had to sit down on a bench while I finished talking to him. I was trying to be thrifty with my money while still surrounding myself with luxury. Patrick had taught me well in my six years with him and I was grateful for it.

Hopefully, I would be able to celebrate tonight, maybe with Sam. At least, that was what I told myself on the way home. I took a nap, a shower, and as a force of habit, lubed myself before getting dressed. An expensive linen shirt and a very nice pair of dress shorts with sandals seemed to be the way to go. I drove to Waipani and climbed the stairs to their unit. Knocking on the door, I waited, holding my breath.

Michael answered with his boundless energy. "Brand! Come in."

"Thank you, Michael," I said as I moved into the condo, spotting Sam and his father right away.

"Brand, this is our dad, Cam," Sam said. Sam looked super cool in a tight t-shirt that showed off his muscular chest and arms, and striped cargo shorts. My senses were overwhelmed with the sight and smell of him.

I held my hand out to shake while Cam scrutinized me.

That was okay, because I was doing the same to him. He was just as tall as Sam with the same wavy blond hair, cut short. He had a full blond beard and kind eyes.

"Hello, sir," I said.

"Hey. These two have been doing nothing but talking about you for days now. I'm glad I get to finally meet you."

He turned to Michael. "Are you ready to go, Mikey?"

"Yes, dad." He groaned.

"Good. I want to talk to Brand for a minute. Why don't you go down to the car, turn it on, and get the air conditioning cranking for us, so it will be nice and cool when we come down?" He held out a keychain and jangled it.

Smart. What teenager didn't want to mess around with a car, and it would get him to leave us alone for a minute or two. Michael took the bait and grabbed the keys on the way out of the door.

"So," I said as I took a seat. Sam sat down beside me and Cam sat down on the opposite couch.

Cam looked me in the eyes and asked bluntly, "You two fucking?" as he waved his pointer finger between Sam and I.

I didn't bat a lash. "No, sir."

Cam stared at me for a second. "I can tell that you're not lying."

"Why would I lie?" I asked as I crossed my legs and leaned back into the couch. Sam was very uncomfortable next to me.

Cam changed tactics. "What are you planning to tell Michael?"

"I thought he had some questions that he wanted to ask me. I suppose that I will just answer him as honestly as I can." I could feel Sam's emotions without even looking at him, as he cycled through them. We were connected in some way that I didn't understand.

"We would like you to check with us before answering," Cam said, smiling.

"How would I do that?"

"We can nod or shake our heads," Sam told me.

"Why don't you just tell me now what subjects are off-limits." I added under my breath, "Like I can't figure it out."

"It's the sex, of course," Sam said, trying to mitigate the discomfort in the room.

"But that's what being a Servant is all about, Sam. It's like telling someone that they are going to be a great painter, but not telling them about paints or brushes."

"It's not the same," Cam said, flatly.

"It is. I should know." I let out a big sigh. "I'm not going to fight with you. Michael is your son and you can do whatever you want with him, but I can tell you that if he enters The Service as a naïve shy kid, he is going to be eaten alive."

Sam looked at his father and said, "Dad, Brand's right about that. He has to be prepared and ready, mentally and emotionally," Sam said, arguing my point.

When Cam didn't say anything, I added, "Cam, I guarantee you that Michael already knows a whole lot about sex, despite your efforts to shelter him. He may even be planning to gain some experience on his own. I know I did."

Cam looked horrified and put his head in his hands, saying, "I know, you're probably right. But I just feel he's still a little too young."

"It's what all fathers feel," I said, understandingly.

He looked up with watery eyes. "We've kept him waiting too long already. Let's go eat." We stood, and Cam put his arm around my shoulders, directing me out the door. "I appreciate you doing this for us, Brand."

"No problem. My pleasure." Plus, it's time with Sam, I added to myself in my head.

Cam drove to Calabash with Michael in the front seat. Sam and I watched each other in the back, wanting to talk, but not daring to. I wanted to jump him right there in the car. The sexual tension between us was thick and hot.

Cam decided on the Dockside for dinner, and we had to wait for twenty minutes for a table. I suggested that we go down to the docks and watch the shrimp boats come in until our table was ready.

Michael and Cam walked ahead, and it gave Sam and me a chance to talk.

"Thanks for doing this. Sorry my dad came off so aggressively," Sam said, with a look that told me that he had been the brunt of his father's aggression before.

"I wasn't surprised. Were you?"

"No."

"On the other hand, your condo smells like you, and I almost popped a boner while I was in there," I said, flashing a coy smile.

"Shut up!" he said, starting to laugh.

"Hand to God!" I laughed back.

Suddenly he looked serious. "Do I have a smell?"

I laughed again. "Yes, and it is intoxicating to me."

He smiled and put his open palm on my nose and grabbed me around the shoulders like he was trying to smother me. I laughed and elbowed him in the side, noticing that his father was watching us. We calmed ourselves down and joined Michael, looking out over the inlet waterway while Cam stared at us.

Our buzzer went off, indicating that our table was ready. We got seated and ordered as I decided to get this party started. I barely even noticed the looks we were getting from the other patrons. It was unusual to see one marked man, let alone two of them eating together.

"So, Michael, I heard you have some questions," I said.

"A lot." He smiled.

"Well, fire away."

"When did you enter The Service, Brand?"

"I was sixteen when I left for The Service Academy and eighteen when I was called for." The hushpuppies had arrived at the table, and the restaurant was famous for them. Cam, Sam, and I nervously chomped away on them while we waited for the next question.

"Did you like the SA?"

"Yes, very much. I met a lot of people that are my good friends now and . . ." I paused and looked at Sam and Cam. "It taught me a lot that helped make my time in Service easier."

Sam nodded at my choice of words.

"And did you really go to your Master in a cage?" Michael asked with big eyes.

"Yes."

"And what was he like, your Master?"

"Patrick was a very nice guy. He treated me with respect and taught me a lot about business and the world."

"Did he, you know, wanna do it all the time?" He glanced nervously at his father.

"He did at first, but then we settled into a routine."

"Oh," Michael said, grabbing a hushpuppy and biting it. Our food came next, and the waiter made sure we had everything we needed.

Michael continued on his line of thought. "What if you don't like your Master or he's . . . ugly?"

"Well, there is a clause in your contract that lets you out of it if your Master is abusive to you. And another clause that lets him out of it if you don't act right, either. As far as ugly, I think you come to an agreement. Patrick was not my ideal man." I looked over at Sam. "But he was okay."

"How many years were you a Servant, Brand?" Cam asked.

"Six."

"And how old are you now?"

"Twenty-four."

"And you earned a million dollars for each year?" Cam was clearly interested in the money, whereas Michael was interested in the sex.

"No. After the first two years, I negotiated with Patrick."

"But you are well-off?"

"Yes." I was not comfortable talking about my money or the contract that Patrick and I had made. It was none of their business.

"And what will you do now?"

I looked back at Sam. "I'm not sure. What city do you live in, Sam?"

The look of horror on his father's face was priceless.

Sam's smile told me that he was either enjoying me teasing his father or excited by what I was saying, or both. "I live pretty close to here in Lake View."

"Good God! Really? What do you do there?"

"Construction."

"Sam works for dad," Michael said. "You know Lake View?"

"Sure. When I was a kid, my dad would take us the back way through all the little small towns in South Carolina when we made a trip north. It is still my favorite way to come to the beach. I believe we always got ice cream at the Dairy Maid in Lake View, and I would buy hot ginger ale across the street at the gas station."

"Yep. They are both still there."

Michael said, "Hey Brand, did your Master ever tell you to do something that you didn't want to do?"

"Yes, but with Patrick, I was lucky that we could talk about it and sometimes negotiate."

"I hope my Master is like that," Michael said with a sigh.

"I do, too, and maybe your Master will be famous."

Michael's face lit up with excitement. "Do you think he will be?"

"A lot of my friends were Servants to actors, sports stars, celebrities, etc."

"Was your Master famous?"

"Only in his own circle."

"That would be so cool!" Michael gasped.

"Let's not get ahead of ourselves," Cam said, taking another bite of flounder.

Michael took a breath before asking the next question. "Did you fall in love with him, Brand?"

"No."

Michael looked deflated.

"But some of my marked friends have or did." He lit back up again, which told me that he was in it for love. I was, too, at first, but when I didn't find it, I was in it for the money.

"Dad, close your ears," Michael said. "Did you have sex before going to the SA?" he whispered.

"Yes." I saw the look of panic on Sam's face and his father's disapproval. "But I regretted it afterwards. I wasn't ready for it, and I didn't get to know the person like I should have." The shadow of panic left Sam's face and I saw Cam nod to himself as he took another bite.

"What happened?" Michael's face was all concern for me.

"He used me." I saw the look of horror on Michael's face, the look of anguish on Sam's face, and the look of satisfaction on Cam's. I refused to be cowed by it, so I held my head up.

"I'm sorry, Brand," Michael said with genuine concern.

We were finished with dinner, so Cam said, "Dinner is on me. Let's get out of here." We all got up and I watched the heads of most of the patrons turn to us.

"Do you ever get used to the stares?" Michael whispered to me.

"Not really. Sometimes you can tune them out for periods of time."

Michael smiled at me and bounded up to the cashier to see if his dad would buy him some gum. Sam put his big hand on the small of my back and ushered me through the door and outside. It was an intimate act, and I was shocked he had done it in a public place. Maybe he'd had a change of heart. He didn't say anything, but I caught him looking at me twice when I wasn't looking at him.

Cam and Michael joined us at the car and I said, "Ice cream is on me, as long as we can go to Painter's."

"You're on," Cam said, and pulled into the humid night.

At Painter's, Michael whined to his dad that he wished they didn't have to leave tomorrow, and Sam seconded that.

"You know I have to get back to work," Cam said flatly.

"Michael and Sam can stay with me next week. I have that big house all to myself," I offered.

Michael and Sam's faces lit up with excitement. Michael was first to speak. "Can we, dad?"

Sam didn't let him answer. "You said work was slow and you probably weren't even going to have any work for me."

"I don't know. We'll talk about it."

Apparently, that ended the discussion for the time being, since both boys went quiet. We sat in silence and finished our cones.

CHAPTER NINE

When we pulled into the Waipani parking lot and unloaded, Cam shook my hand, told me how much he enjoyed meeting me, and thanked me for helping Michael. His eyes flashed between Sam and me but he didn't say anything. Michael high-fived me and asked if he would see me on the beach tomorrow.

I answered, "Yes."

Sam looked at his dad and said, almost defiantly, "I'm going to walk Brand home."

"Okay," Cam said, pleading him with his eyes not to do it.

I personally didn't know what the big deal was, since my car was only twenty feet away or so. Cam and Michael said their good nights and headed up the stairs.

"Follow me," Sam commanded, and turned on his heel.

I loved when he used that voice and told me what to do! The fire was lit in my crotch and I could feel that familiar tingle in my balls that told me that my cock was going to get hard.

We walked around the pool, down by the outdoor shower and through the walkway to Ocean Boulevard, just as if we were walking to my beach house. Sam waited for me at the road and then turned and walked towards Cherry Grove.

"I want to swim with you in the pool before I have to leave tomorrow," he explained.

"Didn't we just pass the pool?" I asked, confused.

"I don't want Michael or dad to see, so we have to enter from the other side."

I got it then. We circled the pool and entered through the far door.

"Are we swimming in our underwear?" I asked, innocently.

"I'm not," he whispered as we snuck into the back gate. We hid behind the cabana and Sam started to take his clothes off, draping them over a chair.

Was I really going to get to see his cock? After all of the fantasizing about it, I hoped it would not disappoint. I slowly started to take my clothes off, my focus never leaving Sam. His body never failed to disappoint me, and I drank him in with my gaze, constantly thirsty for more. When he dropped his boxers, I saw his cock for the first time and was blown away.

Sam's cock was huge. Granted he was already hard, but it was long and thick like a tree trunk. It was so long and thick that I couldn't believe I had never seen it through his bathing suit. I pulled my boxer-briefs off and my own longer-than-average cock was standing at attention, too, but looked vastly inferior to his.

"Wow!" I breathed, looking at his magnificent tool again.

"Worth the wait?" Sam laughed as he slid into the pool without a splash.

I followed him and, when I came up out of the water, whispered, "Yes."

"Let's stay behind this palm tree barrier, so they can't see us," Sam whispered to me as he pulled me over to him. I loved his hands on me, and my cock responded by growing even harder. His back was up against the side of the pool, and he pulled me into him with his big arm. I loved how comfortable he was with my body.

I didn't want to hesitate once Sam gave me an opportunity, so I pounced on it. I floated right onto his chest, wrapping my legs around his hips. We were eye to eye, and my hard cock was pressed into his abs. I could feel his cock pressing onto my ass crack, and despite the coolness of the water, I could feel his heat. I put each of my hands on his hard biceps and smiled up at him.

"You really want to do this?" I asked.

"Do what?" he asked with a raised eyebrow.

"I just don't want you to regret it."

"Trust me! I'm not going to regret it." Sam's voice was husky with lust.

I reached back behind me in the water and wrapped my hand around his hard tool. It was hot to the touch, despite the cool water, and hard as steel. I rubbed my ass crack against it and heard him moan in response. Finally, I lifted up and balanced my puckered hole on his beautiful cock head.

"You can't," he said, concerned.

"I can."

"You'll hurt yourself."

I raised an eyebrow. "Someone is pretty full of himself . . ."

He frowned. "I just know that when I go to a Service Station, sometimes I have to wait while they scramble to find someone who can take it."

"I can take it," I said confidently as I pressed myself down on him. Sam's cock head burst through my anal ring and stretched it wide as I pushed myself down on it. My eyes teared up as the pain shot through me, feeling like someone had stabbed me in the ass. I had to pause and let my ass get used to his assault.

In a moment of incredible tenderness, Sam wrapped his big arms around me and pulled me into his big chest. He pushed my head onto his shoulder and whispered, "We don't even have any lube."

"I pre-lubed," I said into his shoulder.

"So, you planned this?" He smirked.

I pulled back so I could look at him. "I hoped."

"Well, then it should be easy," Sam said, as he continued to smirk.

The stabbing pain was going away, so I pushed again and a large part of his shaft found its way inside me. He was filling me up like I had never been before. For the first time in my life, I felt like I was completely out of control, spiraling around and around on a giant corkscrew. I pushed down one more time while Sam stroked my back under the water and the rest of his cock plowed into me.

Putting my head back onto his shoulder, I said, "Just give me a minute."

He whispered into my hair, "Would this be a bad time to tell you how fantastic your ass feels?"

"There's never a bad time to hear that." I laughed. "Your big cock is something special, too."

"Thanks. I'm pretty proud of it." He laughed. "But seriously, I just wanted to thank you for what you just did for Michael." I pulled back again to look into his eyes. "I was really nervous about it, but you handled it so well, and I was proud of you."

"Well, thanks, Sam. I enjoyed it, but not as much as I'm enjoying this." And before he could say anything, I put my feet on the tiled pool wall and pushed up, lifting myself off of part of him and then pushing off the concrete lip to impale myself on him again.

"Holy fuck." Sam groaned.

The pain in my ass from his giant tool was slowly starting to subside, and the feelings of pleasure were outnumbering the feelings of pain, so I set a pace to piston up and down on him. The water churned around us and the look of total contentment on Sam's face was so worth the wait. He was such a nice guy, and I was lucky as hell to get to spend his last night with him. The fact that his cock fit in my ass like it belonged there didn't hurt either.

"You feel so fucking good in there," I whispered to him as I continued my assault on his cock.

"Well, let's get it all the way in there, then!" Sam said excitedly. He put his hands on each of my ass cheeks under the water, separated them, held them apart, and thrust his hips forward, driving that cock into me like the wooden pole of a butter churn. And I couldn't wait for Sam's butter.

Wrapping my arms around Sam's thick neck, I laid my head on his shoulder, facing him. I could feel each one of his muscle groups flexing with power as he drove himself into me repeatedly. It was like riding a stallion that was meant for this one task. He was fucking tearing me up, and the water didn't seem to matter to him at all.

"So fucking tight," Sam whispered to me.

I could do nothing but moan back at him. I had fucked a lot of NOMARs in my time, but Sam was putting them all to shame. This fuck was like the ones I had dreamed about before I entered The Service and, in a sudden moment of clarity, I realized that this man might be the man I had dreamed about all my life.

Sam's dick exploded with all the force of a cherry bomb going off. When he busted his nut deep inside me, he shook with the spasms and I rode the waves like the first time I met him.

"Oh, fuck," I whispered.

"It's so hard to stay quiet while I'm fucking up into your ass."

I moved my ass up and down on his sensitive cock, milking it with my ass muscles as he shook from the sensations running through his body. "Fuck me! Why didn't we do this a week ago?" I asked.

Sam burst out laughing and said, "We should have." His breathing was still ragged.

"We can try to make up for it."

"How's that?"

I snorted. "We can go again."

"You already ready for more?"

"Yes, sir." I could feel that his cock hadn't really shrunk very much, and I was definitely hungry for more.

A low growl escaped his lips when I called him *sir* and he immediately said, "Me, too."

He pulled me off his lap and pressed me face first into the tiled wall. He held my arm pinned to the dip in my lower back as he spread my legs with his foot. I was so hot for this man, and everything that he was doing was pushing all my buttons. He used his other hand to slap across my mouth and gag me.

When I felt his cock head at my back door, I was absolutely on fire for him and moaned into his palm. He pushed his hips forward and his big piston split me in half as he plowed into me. This time, at least, I had his last load of cum inside me to help lubricate the path. I groaned hard into his hand and heard Sam moan in pleasure behind me.

One more strong push and he buried his cock to the nuts in me. I felt like his whole arm was up inside me and I was his puppet. I arched my back and tilted my head back towards him.

Sam whispered in my ear, "Okay?"

I nodded, and I could just picture him smiling beside my ear. Sam wasted no time setting a terrific pace. He held me in his iron grip, completely at his mercy, using my body to satisfy his every lustful need, and I was perfectly content with that. I wasn't sure what was happening to me, but it felt perfectly natural to let Sam have dominion over me.

Sam was fucking my ass like it needed to be fucked, and I couldn't even begin to imagine what tomorrow would be like without him. I didn't want to think about that, so I banished it from my mind. I rode the wave of pleasure and exhilaration that Sam was giving me and used my tongue to lick his palm.

"No, no, no," he whispered into my ear, his cheek and lips grazing my neck and ear, sending waves of stimulating pleasure coursing through me like the fireworks on the Fourth of July.

Stopping my tongue, I wanted nothing more than to please him. For the first time in my life, I was helpless. Not only helplessly being fucked, but helpless to control how I felt about this man who was fucking ripping me another one from behind, and helpless to stop him from leaving tomorrow.

"Jesus, how is your hole so tight? I've fucked a hole at the Service Station before and the second time I go to fuck it, it's always loose and not as good. But your ass is tight as hell." Sam sounded perplexed.

I couldn't answer with his hand over my mouth, so I moaned and pushed my ass further back onto his root.

"I love that you can't get enough of me," he whispered, driving me out of my mind. "And I love that you can't use your smart mouth right now." Sam started to chuckle in my ear.

The water started to splash as Sam increased his pace and did his best to punch a permanent hole in my ass. He grunted under the effort, eventually releasing my arm, but still holding me tightly against the wall with his chest and stomach. His deep thrusts were starting to lift me off my feet with his power and my lightness in the water.

When I heard his breathing become shallow and his cock twitch inside me, I knew Sam was close to releasing another load of hot spunk inside me. I did everything I could to squeeze his dick with my ass muscles, but he was so fucking big and so fucking hard that I didn't have too much success.

"I'm coming in your sweet ass again," he whispered. Sam inserted three big fingers into my mouth and hooked my head, turning it towards him. I didn't know if he wanted to see my face, but I wanted to see his. I saw him with one eye and simultaneously sucked his thick fingers as if they were his cock. So many things were running through my mind, and there were so many things I wanted to do to Sam's body.

I loved the look on his face when he fell over the edge of his climax and exploded with a torrent of hot semen inside me. Sam continued to thrust into me, enjoying the sensations that came with his climax. My cock was pressed against the cool tile wall and suddenly I found myself coming, as well.

"I'm coming, too," I mumbled around his fingers.

Sam immediately pulled me off the wall, reached down, and stroked my hard cock. "Let me see it," he commanded.

I did as I was commanded and let loose my load into the dark water. Sam, whose cock was still buried in my ass, lifted me up with his hips so that my cock head appeared above the waterline. Long strands of ghostly white cum shot out onto the tiled wall in front of me.

"Good boy." Sam stroked me, removing his fingers from my mouth and his body off me.

"And exactly how old are you, Sam?" I asked, quietly.

"Twenty-three."

"Uh-huh," I said with attitude.

"I knew I should have kept that smart mouth covered longer," he said with a snort.

"Oh, the things I can do to you with this smart mouth," I said suggestively.

"I wish."

I pulled myself off his cock and turned around toward him, wrapping my legs around his waist.

"Sam, seriously, I want you to talk to your dad about letting you stay here next week. I know he probably won't let Michael stay, but at least we could have some more time together."

"I'm going to do it." I could see in his eyes that he was

committed to it.

"I mean, if you want to," I quickly added.

Sam grabbed my face in both of his hands. "I would never disrespect you like that asshole that you had sex with before going to the SA. When you told that story tonight, it broke my heart. Believe me, even though we just fucked, I want to spend as much time with you as possible."

This was the most expressive I had ever heard him.

"I would never use you."

"Unless I asked you to." I smirked.

"Man, I hope we get to that day soon." He smiled, dazzling me with his bright teeth reflected in the security lights around the pool.

"Me, too."

Sam was the perfect man for me, and I couldn't believe that I was lucky enough to have found him while on vacation. We used our clothes to dry ourselves off before departing the way we came in. Between the chlorine and the cum, I smelled strongly of bleach, and I was glad I had put an extra beach towel in the trunk of my car. I used it to cover my seat before sitting down. The pain erupted through me as my sore asshole hit the seat and I winced from it.

"I'll see you tomorrow," Sam assured me, not noticing my look of pain.

"Will you?"

"Of course. Dad will be pissed about this, but I'm going to have a heart to heart with him."

"Good luck," I said, not feeling much hope.

"Come to the beach tomorrow morning."

"What time?"

"Eight. We have to leave by eleven."

"Thanks for taking the chance on me, Sam."

"Welcome. Now, go home."

"And dream of you?"

"Of course. I know I won't be able to stop thinking about you or your remarkable ass."

"You are too kind, sir."

"I mean it, go!" he ordered.

"Yes, sir!" I smiled and pulled out of the parking lot.

CHAPTER TEN

I woke up early, having slept like a baby. If all I had to do to get a good night's sleep was to get fucked by Sam, then sign me up for constant fucks. I toasted a bagel and grabbed a glass of juice before packing my beach bag and heading down to the car.

It was exactly eight when I walked onto the beach. It took me a couple of seconds to spot my boys, but fortunately the beach was mostly empty due to most renters having to leave today and, of course, the early hour. They only had chairs and towels, just like me. Michael was almost to the water and Sam had just left the chairs, following him. That would leave just Cam and me to chat when I put my stuff down. Lucky me.

"Hi, Cam," I said, opening my chair.

"Hey, Brand." I tried to read the emotions on his face or in his tone of voice, but I guess Sam had inherited his poker face from his father, because Cam was as blank as a statue.

I attempted some small talk. "You guys get all packed this morning?"

"Yeah, we're ready to go."

"Good." I folded my towel over the back of my chair, took my t-shirt and flip-flops off, and sprayed myself with sunscreen. I noticed that Cam's gaze never left my body.

"Listen, Brand. I don't want to mince words with you. I don't like . . . what you and Sam are doing. I think it's a mistake, but I guess it's a mistake you two have to make."

God, where was he going with this?

Cam continued, "But I appreciate what you did for Michael

last night and I think you handled it better than I ever thought anyone could. And I have watched you interact with Sam and Michael, and you are good with them both. And you are respectful of me."

I found myself nodding my head foolishly.

"And I have to come to the conclusion that you are a very good person. My Sam wouldn't give you the time of day otherwise. I am confident of that. The bottom line, Brand, is that I like you." He paused or cut it off awkwardly.

When I saw that he wasn't going to say anything else, I said, "Well, thanks, Cam. I like you, too. And I do like Michael and Sam, a lot."

"Very good," he said with finality.

"I'm going to the water."

"Enjoy," he said, dismissing me.

I turned towards the water and saw that Sam was standing just at the tide's edge, watching Cam and me. He must have known this little talk needed to happen, but looked concerned about it. The sight of him made my legs weak. His tall muscular bronzed body was glistening in the morning sun, and my crotch came alive at the sight of it. I remembered our time together last night and blushed as I walked. My ass itched and burned at the memory of him long-dicking me into submission.

"Hey," Sam greeted me cautiously.

"Hey." I saw Michael riding waves from the deep and we started walking towards him. "Thanks for last night, Sam. It was really, really terrific."

"You deserved it," he said, with lustful passion coloring his voice. "I bet you probably have had a lot of experiences just like it, though."

"Never," I stated firmly. "It might have been the most amazing two fucks of my life," I admitted as I blushed.

"Really? Are you paying for it today?"

"Kinda, but it was so worth it." I was a little disappointed that Sam hadn't agreed with me on this fact.

"I thought you were walking a little gingerly," he said, grinning out of the side of his mouth, which I found to be super-sexy. We were almost to Michael in the deep water, and I was grateful that my hard-on was no longer visible. "You had a talk with my dad?"

"Yeah. Not what I was expecting. He said he liked me. I guess he knows about us."

"Hey, Brand," Michael said with enthusiasm when he saw me.

"Hey, guy. You're riding those waves like a champ." He beamed at me and took the next one in.

Sam seamlessly continued our conversation from before Michael's interruption. "I told him last night when you went home. He was waiting for me and accused me of fucking you immediately."

"Really?" I felt bad for him.

Sam smiled at me and said, "He said he could smell you on me."

"Well, I certainly did smell last night."

Michael re-joined us and we talked a little about his next year of high school and what courses he should take. He was very interested in everything I had to say on the matter and soaked it all in like a sponge. Another big wave rolled in and Michael body-surfed it to the shore.

Sam continued, "I told him that we fucked and it was the most amazing experience of my life."

I was taken aback by this news, so all I could do was stare and smile at him.

"And I told him that I didn't regret it at all," Sam finished.

"No, me either."

"And I told him that if you would still have me, that I was going to stay with you for another week."

"Holy Shit, Sam!" My heart leapt into my throat and I leapt into his arms to hug him. I had hoped he would, but honestly didn't expect him to stay.

"He's not going to let Michael stay, but he really can't stop me, and that is what is driving him crazy."

I couldn't stop staring at him as I realized that I was going to get to fuck this amazing man for another week.

"Do you still want me to stay?"

I saw the vulnerability on his poker face and it made my heart melt. "More than anything," I blurted out.

His face lit up with his big smile.

"The most amazing experience of your life?" I smirked with a raised eyebrow.

"It was pretty fucking spectacular . . . wasn't it?" Suddenly he was unsure.

"It was," I said, starting to laugh. "I'm just picking on you."

Sam pushed me away from him and yelled, "Let's ride these waves." I dove under and rode a big wave in. I rode the next one and the three of us had a contest to see who could go the farthest.

Now that I had fucked with Sam and I knew that what I was feeling for him was more than just lust, I had to admit that I enjoyed being with him and with Michael more than ever. They were good people, and I was energized from being around them. We were still laughing when we finally came out of the surf and onto the beach.

When Cam saw us coming, he stood up from his chair and handed our towels to us. "It is time to go, I'm afraid."

"Awww," Michael whined.

Cam said, "Michael, Sam has decided to stay for the next week, since Brand has so graciously offered." The look on Michael's face was aghast with betrayal. Sam's face was wrought with sympathy for his little brother.

Cam continued, "So, I've decided to let you stay as well."

"What?" Michael asked in dismay.

"Really?" Sam asked in astonishment.

I saw the cleverness in it right away. Cam couldn't stop Sam from staying with me, but he could throw Michael into the mix, so that Sam would feel obligated to be a role model and that would keep us apart.

"Yes."

"Oh, thank you, dad. It will be so much fun!" Michael hugged his father, almost knocking him off his feet.

"Thanks, dad," Sam said, also hugging him.

I did not thank him, but stayed silent.

"Michael, you have a doctor's appointment on Thursday, so I will come back and get you on Wednesday after work." Michael looked crest-fallen but clearly had no room to argue. "Uncle Dale and I will come down and bring your truck, Sam, and then the three of us will go back together."

"Sounds reasonable," Sam commented.

"Come say goodbye to me and get your things," Cam told his boys. We gathered our things up and headed to the car. Transferring Sam and Michael's luggage into my car, we said bye to Cam. I shook his hand, told him that it was nice to meet him, and that I looked forward to seeing him again on Wednesday night.

Cam hugged his sons and drove away, waving to them. I noticed that he had whispered something into Sam's ear, and I was very curious as to what it was, but it would have to wait until we were alone again. We piled into my small sports car and drove to the house.

Michael was properly impressed and made all kinds of awe-inspired sounds as he walked around. When we went upstairs, I pointed down the hallway and said, "Michael, you can take any of those bedrooms down the hall." I motioned with my head to Sam to indicate for him to put his things in the master bedroom. I saw him shake his head side to side silently.

Oh, for God's sake.

"Michael, your brother is going to sleep in my room. Are you okay with that?" The look of shock on Sam's face made that familiar burn begin in my crotch.

"Did you guys finally hook up?" Michael asked plainly.

"Michael," Sam said, even more stunned.

"What? You two have been jousting with each other all week. It's about time, Sam. You liked him from the first time we saw him in the water that first day from the boat."

I looked at Sam, and he flushed under my scrutiny.

Michael continued, "Everyone could see that Brand liked you, but you were playing hard to get."

"Wow. He doesn't miss much, does he?" I said to Sam.

"I guess not," Sam answered. "So, it's okay with you if I sleep here."

"Of course." And then he lowered his voice and almost whispered, "Was it good, Brand?"

I looked at Sam to see if I should answer and what I should answer, but he just smiled and raised his shoulders. "It was really good, Michael. Your brother is a very special man."

"Good," Michael said almost absentmindedly as he turned and went down the hallway looking for a good bedroom to claim as his own.

Sam tilted his head to the side and made the weird face that meant *What the fuck!* He put his suitcase in my bedroom and said, "Well, that went well."

"It did, didn't it?"

"I should punish you for asking him that." Sam eyed me suspiciously.

I felt light-headed at the mere mention of my tanned god punishing me. "That could be fun . . ."

"But it was the right thing to do."

"Even though I am dying to get in your pants again, I'm going to go down and make us lunch. Make yourself at home." I headed downstairs and put a tray of bacon in the oven and began to slice some tomatoes. I could hear Sam and Michael talking on the floor above, but not what they were saying. The smell of bacon got them both downstairs quickly.

We ate BLT sandwiches with chips while we sat on the porch and enjoyed the view of the ocean. We decided to go swimming again, but this time we just walked out of my rented house and straight into the water. Now that the cat was out of the bag about Sam and me, I was a bit more affectionate in the water. And my hands were very active under the water. At one point, I had stroked Sam's cock so much that I was pretty sure he couldn't move for risk of Michael seeing his hard-on.

Once we tired of the water, we walked back to the house, dried off, and went inside.

"Michael, we're going to shower and then take a nap," Sam said.

"Feel free to make yourself at home, Michael," I added quickly.

"I'm probably gonna do the same thing, shower and nap. We got up really early today," Michael said, yawning.

"Yeah, we did." I smirked.

Sam and I went upstairs and I said, "Nice job getting us alone."

"I mean it. I'm going to shower and nap," he said with an exaggerated face of innocence, but then started to laugh.

"*You* might, but your cock is going to be in my mouth while you shower and in my ass while you sleep," I said decisively.

"Is that your plan?" he asked, closing and locking the bathroom door behind us.

"It is," I said, as I stripped off my bathing suit and kicked it into the corner of the bathroom and turned on the shower faucets. I moved to my golden god and pulled his bathing suit down carefully, trying to not hurt his magnificent manhood.

"Your cock certainly is a thing of beauty. I didn't get to see it much last night."

"But you got to feel it a lot, didn't you?"

"Yes, sir."

"I do like it when you call me that," Sam growled with a husky voice.

"Then I'll have to do it more often, sir." I wrapped my hand around his big cock, marveling at how my big hand could not totally encircle it, and pulled him into the shower. I squirted shampoo into my hand and begun to scrub Sam's thick blond hair. He wrapped his arms around me, locked his fingers together behind my back, and pulled me flat against him.

I massaged his scalp while he moaned his delight. "How did I get so lucky to find you?"

"Oh, you found me?"

He smiled at me and said, "What can I put in that mouth of yours to keep you quiet? Let me think . . ."

I laughed as I soaped up his armpits, holding his big biceps up so that I could get to them. They were covered in dark blond hair. I ran my hands all over his torso, exploring every little inch. I sucked his tiny pink nipples before dropping down to my knees to pay homage to his big cock.

For the first time, I was getting a good look at Sam's monster, and it was even scarier up close. Coming out of a dark blond bush of hair, his cock was so long it actually arched like a rainbow as it stuck out. It took both my hands to hold it steady at the base as I began to explore it properly with my tongue. I looked up at him, and he appeared mesmerized by my actions. He followed my every move as I licked his velvety-soft cock head and poked the end of my tongue into his piss hole. When I finally licked down the sides from the root to the head, Sam moaned and put a big hand onto the back of my head, urging me to suck him. I pulled on his ball sack while I licked that gorgeous tool.

Sam tasted delicious. His cock had no flaws, as far as I was concerned. Trying to unhinge my jaw, like a snake swallowing a snake, I engulfed him with my mouth. I had experience sucking cock . . .a lot of experience . . . and there was no way I could get him all in my mouth, but I was going to do my best.

I sucked hard, but didn't make much of a dent. Sam didn't seem to mind as he directed and guided my head back and forth on his substantial member. I used my tongue to press down on the bottom vein of his cock while I sucked on him. Finally, he held my face in place with both hands and fucked into my open mouth.

Grunting with the exertion of it, Sam finally stopped moving and exploded in my mouth. I backed almost all the way off him, swallowing as fast as I could. His cum was delicious and I savored every drop I could get. He put his head back and enjoyed me continuing to suck on his sensitive cock while he came down from his high.

"Fuck, that's good," Sam said softly.

"Better than good." I smiled as I stood up.

Sam squirted shampoo on his palm and started to massage it into my scalp. I loved his big hands on me, and I luxuriated in his touch. He scrubbed my neck and then my body. For a NOMAR, he was quite thorough in his inspection of my body. He had gone silent on me and was in what I had decided to call *Master Mode*.

Sam twirled me in the water to rinse me by spinning my hips with his hands. He turned the water off, bent down, wrapped his arms around my lower back, and lifted me up onto him. I wrapped my legs around his waist, and he carried us out of the shower, not even stopping to dry off. He placed my wet back on the bed, grabbed the bottle of lube next to the bed, squirted it directly on his wet cock, and lifted my legs up onto his broad shoulders. He used one hand to guide his cock to my hungry hole and slapped the other one across my mouth.

It seemed that whenever Sam went to fuck me, there was always someone nearby that we had to be quiet for. That worked for me. It turned Sam into *Silent Master,* which caused him to gag me while he fucked me, so I seemed to be the winner all the way around.

Sam pushed his hips forward, and his giant cock split me like a rail. It pushed in, filling me all along the length of my anal channel. The searing pain felt like he had inserted a hot knife inside of me instead of his hard column of flesh. The two fit together so well, it felt as if my ass had been formed around Sam's cock. I arched my back and I groaned behind his palm while also lifting my ass slightly so that he could slide one more inch in.

Once Sam was buried to the nuts inside me, he bent forward, bending me in half, and held himself there, hovering over me. My gaze was full of him as he dominated me from above. He stared into my eyes, raising an eyebrow as if to check to see if I was okay.

I nodded behind his hand, and he begun pistoning out of me and then back in. Slowly at first and then steadily building, he worked his baton like a maestro in front of a seventy-two piece orchestra. Sam fucked with such control that it was easy to think that he wasn't into it, but I could feel his pulse quicken in his hand and I could hear his breath growing shallow.

I ran my hands over his strong sides and muscular chest, pinched his little nipples, and rubbed his thick neck. I knew that he was just as excited as I, which was saying something because my cock felt like it was a Roman candle, ready to be lit.

"Fuck!" Sam roared as he came with the force of a sandblaster inside me, spraying hot cum all over the inside of

my ass. I slapped my hand over his mouth, muffling the last part of his vocal eruption, just as I reached my own climax. I came in rapid quick bursts that puddled my cum between our two wet chests. We continued to fuck, each one of us holding our hands over the other's mouth, riding the wave of our orgasms.

Chapter Eleven

Sam and I didn't get to nap at all that afternoon, basically because I couldn't keep his penis out of my ass or mouth. It was the most fun I had ever had on a bed with someone, and when Sam told me that we had to stop and go downstairs, it almost crushed me.

"Let's go," he commanded, and I was powerless to resist. When I stopped playing with him, he smiled and said, "I think I really like this commanding thing."

"I bet you do." I smirked. Walking down the stairs, I could hear the TV and saw that Michael was already up from his nap.

"Hey guys. How was your nap?" He used air quotes on the word *nap*.

"Very relaxing," I said, heading to the kitchen and feeling my asshole burn with every step. Each second reminded me of my *nap* with Sam and I smiled to myself as I secretly enjoyed it.

"Can we go ride the waves?" Michael asked, turning the TV off.

"Sure," Sam said.

"You guys go ahead. I'm going to mix this mac and cheese for dinner and put it in the oven, and then I'll come out."

"Awesome," Michael said, running out to the porch.

Sam came over, pressed himself up against my back, and whispered in my ear, "Do you want me to wait for you?" I could feel his almost rock-hard cock pressing into my ass crack through both of our bathing suits.

I reached behind me, grabbed his cock through the fabric and said, "Wasn't three times enough?"

He considered me for a moment with his bronze-tinted eyes. "Was it enough for you?"

"No."

He smiled immediately, his concern erased.

"You go with Michael. I won't be long, but I see you will be," I smirked.

"As I recall, you really like me being long."

"I certainly do," I said, starting to laugh as I turned back to making the mac and cheese. I finally finished it, put it in the oven on low heat, and set the alarm on my phone, which I put in a plastic Ziploc baggie and took with me to the beach.

Playing with Michael and Sam in the water was fun, and they enjoyed my section of the beach for not being as crowded as where they were used to going. I checked my phone after riding a wave to the shore and saw that I only had a few minutes before the dinner was ready, so I waved to the boys, dried off, and headed inside.

I made a big salad to go with the pasta and set the table before Sam and Michael came inside.

"It smells fantastic in here," Sam said.

"It will be ready in a minute," I said. I was still waiting for the garlic bread to finish.

Michael had run upstairs to change, so Sam said, "Who knew you were such a good cook?"

"I have a lot of skills," I said suggestively.

"Yes, you do," he agreed, squeezing my ass cheeks with a big hand. "I'm going to change."

"Can you take all of these bottles of lube with you when you go?" I asked, handing him several bottles that I had hidden. "I don't think we want Michael to see all of this."

"Wow. What were you doing before we got here?" I could tell that he was half-kidding and half-serious.

"Waiting on you to show, if I remember correctly," I bantered back. "Besides, with the way we are going, we will probably use all of those bottles in the next few days."

"Touche. I was a fool for not coming to you earlier."

I turned and looked into his face and saw that he regretted it. "It made our pool swim even more fantastic, didn't it?"

"Hell, yeah, it did." He grinned from ear to ear as he walked upstairs carrying the bottles.

We ate, played cards, and watched a movie the rest of the night. Michael, like a typical teenager, wanted to stay up all night, but I was ready for bed after the movie.

"I'm tired. I'm going to head up," I announced at the end of the movie.

"You better join him, Sam, or you'll be in trouble," Michael said, snorting and laughing.

I rolled my eyes at Michael, but Sam didn't hesitate, getting up and saying, "Goodnight."

My mouth watered at the thought of what was coming, and that itch deep in my ass made its presence known all over again as I climbed the stairs. Neither Sam nor I had showered after the ocean except for the outdoor shower, so when he climbed onto the bed naked with me, I pushed him down flat, straddled him, and sat down on his abs, I couldn't wait to lick his salty skin.

Sam was starting to grow a beard, so I started with his earlobe, gently sucking it into my hot mouth as I leaned over him. I ran my tongue around his ear and then down his jaw line, enjoying the sharp prickly hairs of his stubble. Then I licked and sucked his meaty neck, unable to get enough of it. His hands constantly moved over my back, sides, and ass as I worked. His collarbone was next, and I explored it with a hungry tongue before moving down to his small tan nipples. Biting, sucking, licking, and teasing were standard torments that I reserved for those delicious little nubbins.

Sam groaned and pushed his chest into my face and his nipple further into my mouth. I slid back onto his legs and continued my licking to his hairy armpits, making broad swipes with my extended tongue before licking down his sides, onto his abs, and stomach. My tongue flicked into his bellybutton, which was just as cute as it could be. Sam's hands were constantly on me, following my descent.

Next I moved on to his cock, licking and sucking to both of our delights. I got the extra bonus of some of his pre-cum, which he started to produce as I worked him over. It was the nectar of the gods and I sucked as much of it down as he produced. I moved my tongue down to his ball sack, licking for my life. His sack was smooth and small, compared to his cock, but just the right size for my mouth. I was able to put both of his balls and his bag into my mouth and roll them around. I followed the seam of his ball sack from his grundle to the base of his cock.

It must have been very exciting for Sam, because his breath caught and he stared down his chest at me in disbelief. I continued to manipulate his balls before slowly spitting them out, one at a time, and moving onto the licking of his inner thigh. His knees were next, and I enjoyed the salty sweat that I found behind them, before moving on to his lower legs and then to the treat that I had been waiting on since the first day that I had seen him.

I was completely off the bed now, kneeling at the end of it. I lifted one big foot and licked his ankle and then down the top of his foot. Sam's eyes were wide and his mouth was O-shaped as he watched me. He had some of his dark blond hair on his feet and I ran my tongue along the top of each toe before turning to the bottom.

I smiled up at Sam as I ran my thumb hard across the bottom of his feet. "You know, this is the first part of you I saw."

"What?" His voice broke.

"When you were in the inflatable boat with Michael, I only saw the bottoms of your big feet. I knew right away that they were for me. I saw them again later on the first day we met when you rode the wave away from me, leaving me with just this view."

"You have a thing for feet?" he asked, almost not believing me.

"I have a thing for *your* feet." I smirked, then ran my big tongue on the bottom of those white pads from the heel to the toes.

"God damn," Sam said, throwing his head back and opening his mouth.

I sucked all of his toes into my mouth, and then only one toe at a time, running my tongue between each one. Then I sucked down the side, putting his instep into my mouth and then the heel and then the outside edge. I reached up and grabbed his cock which was rock hard and stroked it while I repeated the foot bath for the other foot. Cold lube poured on his hard cock as I stroked it and I looked up to see Sam pouring it onto his cock head.

"Come up here," he commanded, apparently having taken more teasing than he could stand.

"Yes, sir," I said, as I crawled onto the bed, straddled his crotch, and lowered myself down onto his magnificent cock.

He guided his thick monster into my sweet hole while I bent forward, holding myself up with my palms flat on his pecs. Once his cock head had popped through, Sam moved his hands to my ass cheeks, separating and holding them apart. I could feel every inch of his hard cock in this position and it took my breath away. The pain radiated out from my ass along every neural pathway in my body, but he continued to slide that big sea monster inside my dark cave.

Sam bent his knees, driving himself inside me even further

and I straightened up, feeling his cock move inside me. I reached back behind me with both arms and held onto his knees as I felt the pain in my ass turn to pure pleasure.

"This is the first part of you that I saw." Sam grinned at me.

I pulled my head forward in surprise and asked, "What, my chest?"

"No. Your face. Your face just now had the same look of sheer pleasure on it that your face held that first day in the water while you were riding the waves." Sam ran his flat palm up my stomach and chest.

"You noticed that?" I asked, stunned.

"I noticed everything about you. Now, be quiet so I can get my fuck on," he said snarkily.

Sam held my face in his big hands as he fucked me hard from below while I rode him like a bucking bronco. I didn't realize that I was moaning so loudly until he rammed his sword to the hilt in me, held me still, and slapped his hand over my mouth. I looked down at him, and he had his finger from his other hand on his lips.

I listened with all my might and thought I could hear sounds on the steps. I turned back to Sam and then we both heard the sound of Michael's bedroom door shutting. Sam's cock was throbbing inside me, beating like his heartbeat.

"Thank God," I whispered into Sam's ear. "I need that cock to get back to work."

Laughing also, his facial hair scratching my cheek as his lips moved to my ear, Sam said, "Not as much as I need it to." He began to slowly thrust into me, constantly increasing the speed, until he was right back to my bucking bronco again. I jacked my cock as he tore me up from below.

Sam squirted a little lube on the head of my cock which was very thoughtful, because now my hand just flew over my hard shaft.

"Come on my chest," Sam ordered me, using his

commanding voice which I knew not to question.

"Yes, sir," I said. I jacked my cock harder, as he slowed his pace in my ass. I was in heaven as I fell over my climax with his giant member buried deep inside me. My cum shot in hot ropy threads across his chest and neck, then dribbled onto his abs.

I leaned forward and licked him clean. I liked the taste of my own cum, but it wasn't Sam's delicious spunk. My tongue ran over his neck and collarbone, vacuuming up the hot cum, as well as licking his salty sweaty skin again.

Sam took the opportunity to finish while I was bent forward. He fucked me with such speed that it felt like my asshole might catch fire. Soon there was cum in my ass as well as my mouth. Sam, at the height of his climax, pulled his cock out of my ass and held it nestled in my ass crack, like a giant ballpark frank in a bun. It spurted like a fountain, his hot seed landing in big raindrops on my back and ass.

I felt his hands holding me down on to his chest, his beard tickling me again. His lips touched my ear as he whispered, "I'm not sure what is happening between us."

"What do you mean?" I asked into his chest.

"I have never felt this way before . . . or had this much sex before."

"Does it bother you?"

"No, I'm ecstatic about it, but I'm not sure why it is happening."

"We're having fun, yes?"

"For sure."

"Then let's just keep having fun, and we will talk about it at the end of the week. And what do you mean that you haven't ever had this much sex before?"

"I haven't." He seemed offended.

"Your stamina is unbelievable. What did you do before you finally gave in to me?"

"I whacked off . . . a lot."

I pulled myself up to look at him in the face. "Did you whack off thinking of me?"

He instantly flushed, "Yes." He averted his eyes.

"Don't worry, I did, too."

"How many times?" he asked me, smirking.

"It would be easier to count the days." I smirked back. We both laughed and I said, "I know you're tired, Sam, since you didn't sleep much last night. I'll try to let you get some rest."

"You don't want to fuck again?"

"Of course I do. I would have you fuck me all night long if I could, but you need your sleep. We've got six more days together, and I want you well-fed and well-rested so that you're on top of your game."

He chuckled so deeply that his chest rumbled, and I bounced on top of it. "And have I not been good at the game, so far?"

"Excellent. Truly excellent." I breathed into his broad chest.

CHAPTER TWELVE

Sam was energetic from getting so much sleep the night before and showed off by fucking me hard in the morning, twice.

I showered, thanking my lucky stars for finding this man even if my ass was constantly feeling the effects of it. Sam was making breakfast, and when he finished, we switched places, working like a well-synchronized team. Michael was in a great mood and asked to go para-sailing today. I was up for it, so I told him that I would ask Sam when he came down.

Sam did come down a little while later and he was all excited for para-sailing, so we were set. Michael ran upstairs to get ready. I took the opportunity to talk with his brother without him listening.

"So, what did your father say to you when he was leaving?"

He thought for a second. "Oh, he said to keep Michael safe."

"From me?"

"From everybody, I think. I guess you are included in that." He smirked.

"You don't seem to need any protection from me," I snarked.

"I might if you don't let me get some rest."

"I did last night."

"Yes, you did."

I grabbed my wallet and we headed to the beach. We had to walk up the beach a little ways to find the para-sailing

106

guys. The price wasn't outrageous, so we signed up. Michael was a little scared and wanted Sam to go tandem with him, but Sam weighed too much.

"I'll go with you, Michael, if you don't mind."

"Cool!"

Sam went first on the single parachute and looked like he was having a blast. I personally enjoyed seeing Sam in his harness, because it left nothing to the imagination. His cock was outlined by those harness straps, just like if I had trussed him up for some S&M play.

Michael decided to use my tactic and talk to me while his brother was out of earshot. "Brand, can I ask you some questions about some things since we are alone?"

I was cautious, but agreed. "Sure."

"When you were with your Master, did he ask you to fuck other men?"

"Yes."

"Do most Masters?"

"I would say that most of them do. Either by watching you fuck someone else, or trading Servants with another Master, or by going to a party with multiple people."

"So, you do have to have sex with a lot of people, not just your Master?"

The para-sail guys gave us harnesses to put on, so we started to step into them and buckle them.

"Yes, usually. But every Service is different, so you may get a Master who only wants you for himself."

He blushed slightly and then looked up at me and asked, "Does Sam only want you for himself?"

"God, I hope so," I said, as I burst out laughing. "Your brother is the bomb!"

Michael flushed further and almost whispered, "There's just a lot of stuff I don't know how to do yet."

"But you want to do, right?"

"Oh, yeah. I want to do it all now."

I laughed at his eagerness. "You will learn how to do most things at the SA."

The para-guys checked our harnesses and strapped us into the double parachute, giving us the instructions on how to take off and land. They were fascinated with two marked guys harnessed together, and I was sure from their hard-ons that they were imagining what they could do to us.

"I don't know if I can wait that long." Michael cringed.

"I felt the same way." My heart was breaking for him. I remembered what it was like, and I was acutely aware of the feelings he was having.

Suddenly the para-guys were counting down and we took off running and then were in the air. It was fantastic! The feeling of hanging in mid-air and the view of the beach was awesome. Michael and I nervously looked for sharks under us in the deeper water, but couldn't distinguish anything. We screamed and high-fived each other, laughing hard.

"How did you tell Sam that you like him?" Michael was talking loudly, but the wind was swallowing his words.

This caught me off-guard for a couple of seconds. "I used my body language—my smile and my eyes, of course."

"You didn't actually tell him?"

"Not at first. I let him come to the conclusion himself first. Then, when he didn't respond, I asked him whether he liked me or not."

He made a shocked face. "Did you?"

"Yes."

"And what did he say?"

"He said that he did, but wasn't sure he wanted to act upon it."

"Why not?" Michael was just full of questions.

This was one I wasn't sure if I should field or not. "He wanted to be a good role model for you, and he wasn't sure what you would think about it."

"Really?" Michael thought to himself for a second. "I think it is the coolest thing he has ever done. I love the way he treats you, how happy he is around you, and how much you two like each other."

"Thanks."

"Seriously though, I bet I can guess when you guys finally fucked. I bet it was Friday sometime. Right?"

"Yes," I admitted.

"I knew it! He was so freaking happy Saturday morning, and we were leaving, I knew it was you. That was the happiest I have seen him since during one of his big football games in high school."

Now it was my turn to be shocked. "Really?"

"Yeah. Not that he has been unhappy or anything, but I could just tell that he wasn't really happy. You know what I mean?"

"Yes." I really did know what he meant. For the past six years, I had been the same way—happy, but not really happy.

"I don't think I will be able to do it," Michael suddenly said.

"Do what?" I had been lost in my own thoughts for a second and had no clue what he was talking about.

"Fuck. Anal, that is."

I dismissed his fears with one phrase. "Of course you will."

"Doesn't Sam's penis hurt you when he puts it in you?"

"Yes, but you compensate and manipulate, so that it becomes pleasurable."

"I've seen Sam's cock, and I don't think it will go inside my little hole." Michael looked at me with all seriousness, so I knew he wasn't yanking my chain. "I mean, sometimes a really big shit hurts me so badly."

"Michael, you know that not all cocks are the size of Sam's, don't cha?"

"Really?"

He was much more naïve than I had earlier thought. "Your brother's cock is the largest one I have ever seen or fucked with. Ninety-nine percent of the men in our world have smaller cocks than him. In fact, I have had sex with a man with a cock as long as your brother's, but never one as wide and never one with both qualities."

"Until now," Michael said with a smile.

"Until now," I agreed. The boat was turning around, which caused us to lose the wind in our parachute, and we began to fall towards the water. We both looked at each other, concerned, and breathed a sigh of relief when the boat sped forward and the rope became taut again, causing us to sail up into the air.

"You will have no problem with most guys. Besides, don't you have a cock that is similar to Sam's? They usually run in families."

"Mine's almost as big as his, but not quite."

"Jesus! You're going to be very popular at the SA."

"Why?" Then his eyes widened suddenly. "Will they make me fuck other guys?"

I smiled. "They won't make you, but a lot of guys are going to ask you to."

He lowered his voice. "Did you
?"

"Of course. I love fucking." He looked down-trodden.

"What's wrong?"

"I just wish I knew how to fuck and suck and be fucked."

I smiled, having felt the same way at his age.

"Do you think you would let me practice . . . with you?" he asked all wide-eyed.

Fuck!

"No, Michael, I don't think that would be appropriate."

He started to whine. "Why not?"

"Well, because I'm interested in your brother, you are way

too young, and your brother and father would not like it."

"Okay, don't tell Sam, okay?"

"I can't do that." I knew instantly that I had to tell him. "He won't be mad."

"He's going to kill me," Michael lamented.

"Isn't there a boy your age at home that you like?"

Suddenly he was shy and flushed, "Yes."

"NOMAR?"

"Yes. Last school year, a couple of older guys asked me to suck them off at my locker one day, and Josh stood up for me and ran them off."

"Sounds like a good guy. Bet he might like to practice with you."

"That's what I was thinking, too, but I don't know how to ask him."

"Use your body language!" I yelled. "And if that doesn't work, just ask him. I guarantee you that he will say yes."

We were being signaled to land, so we pulled on the parachute cords to swing out over the beach, and we dropped farther and farther down until we hit the sand running. It was a weird sensation, kinda like on the verge of being trampled, but we finally stopped, and the para-guys unhooked us. Sam was there to high-five us and asked how we liked it.

All three of us were full of adrenaline and talked about our experience all the way back to the beach house. I could tell something was wrong with Sam, who was constantly grabbing his crotch and walking funny. I prayed to God that he had not pulled a groin muscle.

As soon as we hit the threshold, Sam told Michael, "I need to speak with Brand for a couple of minutes, Michael. Can you wait on the porch for us? And then we'll go swimming and cool off."

"Okay," Michael said, with a look of concern.

I was also concerned as Sam ushered me into the back

bedroom on the first floor. "What's wrong?" I asked before the door was even shut.

Sam didn't answer me at first, but unbuttoned his cargo pants and pulled out his huge member. He was rock-hard and painfully erect. "You gotta help me. It's killing me." The look on his face told me that he was really in pain and not just being opportunistic.

"Sure," I said, dropping to my knees. "Why's it so hard?"

"The adrenaline, I think, or it could have been seeing you trussed up in that harness."

I laughed before sucking him into my mouth. There was no way I could get him all in, but the parts I did have in I treated well. Licking and sucking my way up and down that pole, I pulled on his balls for good measure as I focused all my attention on his thick shaft.

"Hold still," Sam commanded me, as he put both his hands on my head and held me still. "You okay?" he asked me, stopping suddenly.

"Yes, sir." I knew my words would set him even more on fire, and I was rewarded by seeing Sam close his eyes and swallow hard. He reopened them, stuck his thumb in my mouth like a fishhook, and then preceded to face-fuck me with a huge smile on his own face.

I let my tongue and throat do the work for me as Sam pistoned into my mouth over and over. He finally came with great bucking spasms—his load so large that I almost gagged as I tried to swallow as fast as he was pumping his hot cum into me. He continued to mini-thrust into my mouth as I cleaned up his sloppy cock, milking the last little bit of delicious cum out of his fuck-stick.

"Fuck! That's what I needed," Sam told me, breathing heavily. "Thanks, Brand."

"I should be thanking you," I said, as I continued to lick down his shaft like a Popsicle.

"You're always doing everything for me. I'm not using you like that one guy, am I?" Sam's normally cute face wore a mask of horror.

"Fuck no. Why would you even think that?"

"I don't ever want to do that to you. I want us to be partners, equals."

"We are. Don't worry, I will tell you when you are being a dickhead."

He laughed. "I bet you will. I've never met anyone as direct as you."

"I will," I said, standing. "I don't want to leave Michael out there much longer, but I have to tell you something he said to me."

The look of concern was back on Sam's face.

"When we were para-sailing, he told me that he was upset that he didn't know how to suck or fuck or be fucked." The look on Sam's face was steady. He had gone into poker face mode. "He asked if I could teach him or let him practice."

"And what did you say?" Sam's tone was commanding.

"I said no, of course, and I gave him three good reasons."

Sam had that serious look on his face and I didn't know him well enough to know how he was going to react to this news. He finally looked down at me and said, "We have to talk about this more, but let's go out to him."

"We have to put on our bathing suits," I said, opening the door. Sam and I went upstairs to change and came back down to find Michael waiting for us on the porch. He had already changed and had a towel. He was ready to go and seemed to me to be very nervous.

He looked at me, as if asking if I had told. I wasn't sure how to respond. Fortunately Sam put Michael in a headlock and pulled him down the steps. We were all laughing as we raced to the water and into the deep.

Chapter Thirteen

Monday morning, I woke up with Sam wrapped around me like a bear skin blanket. It was fantastic and warm. I usually kept the beach house air conditioner on as low as possible, so Sam's body heat was welcome. Besides the heat, I loved being this close to him, smelling him, feeling his breath on my hair and having his big arm draped over me.

I reached back and grabbed hold of his morning wood. As soon as I touched him, his breathing halted, but he didn't stir. Sam's cock was growing in my hand, and I rubbed the tip of his soft head with my thumb, teasing it even more. Realizing that I was holding my breath, I let it out softly and felt him stir behind me. I smiled into my pillow, knowing what was coming next.

Sam stirred on my side, then slid his arm down my leg, lifting it back and up. I let him move me like a rag doll. He put my leg on top of his and then separated his knees. This very successfully separated my ass cheeks and opened my sweet hole to him. He didn't fail to capitalize on that fact, feeding his hot meat into it.

Thank God I was still lubed from last night and had two of his loads of cum inside me, as well. His cock split my anal ring as he pushed forward. My asshole was pushed inside me as he entered, sending waves of electric blue pain coursing through me—on and on it entered, seeming to never end. The blue turned to purple and then to bright orange tongues of pleasure. I slid my asshole down his shaft, squeezing it with all my might as he filled me up.

I moaned, unable to control it as Sam buried his cock to the nuts inside me. He responded by tunneling his hand under my pillow and putting a long thick finger between my teeth. I bit down on it as Sam started to pull himself back out of me and then thrust back inside. I felt like his finger was a bit in a horse's mouth and Sam was going to ride me for all I was worth.

Sam made a circle with his other hand and began to jack my hard cock with it as he fucked me until he reached his climax, shooting hard thick strands of ropy semen into me. I reached back and grabbed his hip and continued to fuck myself on his pole by pushing back onto it while pulling his hip forward.

"Didn't get enough of my big pole?" Sam asked, his voice husky with sleep.

"The one in my mouth or the one in my ass?"

"I like giving both of them to you."

"I can't seem to get enough of either of them."

"Well, perhaps I haven't tried hard enough, then." I heard the lust in his voice a second before he rolled me onto my stomach and was on top of me. His cock was still buried in my ass, and now I felt it throb away inside me. Sam put his knees outside of mine and laid all of his weight on top of me. "Too much?" he checked with me.

"Never, sir."

"Now you're just asking for it." He growled into my ear, his head pressing mine to the side. Sam ran his rough cheek over mine, sending electric currents running through me. He held his body on mine and begun to undulate his hips up and down, driving that golden spike into my railroad tie over and over.

Sam's weight pressing down on me while his gargantuan cock was drilling me added a whole other level to this fuck. My cock was being fucked back and forth on the sheets, giving me a friction hard-on while Sam's hips continued to work like an oil derrick. His pace was nice, neither fast nor slow. He locked in each thrust with a pause and a crotch bump, just to make sure I felt it.

"I'm coming, sir." I moaned.

Sam reached down and forced his hand between my stomach and the mattress. I lifted up slightly to help him, and soon he had his hot hand wrapped around my hard cock.

"Come now," Sam commanded.

"Yes, sir." I moaned. "Fuck it out of me, sir."

Sam was relentless, constantly moving his cock in and out of me. His hand squeezing my cock, his tool drilling for oil in my ass, and his weight pressing me down was all more than I could take. My climax reached its pinnacle and I plunged over it. My spunk shot out, wracking my body with a spasm as it came. Sam's hand was waiting, and I filled up his big mitt with cum. He continued to milk my cock until I was dry, as well as rhythmically fucking into me.

Finally he pulled his hand out from under me and lifted his cummy hand to my mouth. I reached up with both hands and held his big paw so that I could get my tongue on it. I sucked my own cum off of his bare palm as he continued to fuck me.

"Holy fuck," Sam sighed as he breathed into my ear. I wasn't sure whether it was the fact that he was watching me eat my own cum or the fact that I was licking and sucking his fingers and palm like it was his cock, but the pressure was too great and he couldn't hold out any more.

He grabbed my forehead, pulled my head back, and fucking buried himself in me, rocking me with his spasms. I could feel his spunk filling all the crevices his cock wasn't. I couldn't believe there was any room left and I was proven correct when the excess started to run out of me, pooling between our bodies.

"You are an amazing man," Sam whispered to me.

"You are the amazing one. Sometimes I wonder if I can keep up with you."

"All I know is that this has been an amazing couple of days, and I have you to thank for that."

"You can start thanking me by washing these sheets. They have more cum on them than Charlie Sheen's." We both laughed, and Sam rolled off me and I rolled towards him, being able to look at him for the first time today.

"Good morning, sir."

"Don't get me started again."

"Or what?" I teased.

"You might have to get punished."

"Spoken like a true Master."

"You think of me as a Master?" he asked, shock in his voice.

"No, I think of you as *my* Master." I was shocked at my words even as I spoke them.

"Since when?"

"Since those two fucks." I wanted to look away from his probing eyes so that he couldn't see into my heart, into my soul, but I couldn't break our gaze. He wasn't saying anything, so I nervously continued, "I have waited my whole life to be thoroughly sexually dominated, and I've never met anyone who does it like you do. And for me to like you as a person added to how much I love being around you on top of that, makes you my Master."

When Sam did try to speak, he had to swallow hard first. "You might be my Master, because I am completely enthralled with you. I'll do whatever you want me to . . ."

I slapped him on the middle of his big chest and said, "Make me some breakfast, bitch!" Laughing, I headed to the shower.

It took me a while to get clean, using the shower wand to blast most of the cum off and out of me. I left the shower, did some manscaping, and dried off. When I went to put on my bathing suit, I saw that the bed had been stripped.

It made me smile, showing me that he listened to me and cared about me. I made my way downstairs and saw that I was alone. I wondered where Sam and Michael were, but distracted myself with the laundry for a minute. Sam had stripped the bed and brought the sheets downstairs, but just dropped them on the floor in front of the washer. *Well, at least he was trying.*

I transferred a load of beach towels from the washer to the dryer and started the load of sheets. Just then I heard a commotion, and Sam and Michael came busting into the great room.

Sam saw me and said, "I didn't make you breakfast, but we borrowed your car and went and got Krispy Kreme's for you." He held up the box and smiled a crooked grin at me.

"Thanks, guys," I said to them. Then I grabbed the box and whispered Sam's words back to him in his ear, "You might just have to get punished."

Raising an eyebrow, he licked his bottom lip and stared at me. I smirked and opened the box of doughnuts. There were a half-dozen of my favorites—raspberry-filled and cream-filled, as well as a half-dozen of regulars.

"How did you do that?" I asked, turning to him.

"Did we get it right?"

"Yes, but how?" I didn't remember ever saying which doughnuts were my favorites.

"Michael noticed that you always have fresh raspberries in the fridge, and I guessed that you liked cream-filled." Sam smirked hard as he finished that sentence.

"Pretty good guess." I smirked back. "Thank you. It was very thoughtful, and also for stripping the bed."

"What happened to the bed?" Michael asked, munching on a doughnut already.

Sam looked at me with a panicked look on his face. I replied, "Nothing, I just spilt some Diet Coke on the sheets this morning." Sam's face relaxed and I continued, "Michael, you have any clothes you want me to wash for you? You have to be getting low."

"Yeah. Do you mind?"

"No. Go get 'em for me."

"Thanks, Brand," he yelled, as he ran upstairs munching on another doughnut.

"You are really good to him . . . to us," Sam said.

"You have anything that needs cleaning, Master?" I asked coyly.

"Not yet, but I'll find you when I do." He reached for a doughnut and made sure he nestled his cock into my ass crack as he did it.

"I hope so!" I laughed, pushing back on his big cock with my ass.

He smiled into my ear and whispered, "You can call me Master in the bed if you want, but it sounds a little strange outside of it."

"Is that a command, Master?"

There was a pause while he considered. "It is."

"Yes, sir."

Michael came back downstairs with an armload of clothes that he dumped onto the laundry room floor. Grinning broadly, he re-joined us for another doughnut.

"I guess I won't be going to the beach today," I said, sarcastically. Sam's face fell. "Kidding," I said. I turned on Sports Center and we watched the news for a while until we were motivated to get started out to the beach.

By then the dryer was finished, so I emptied it out and threw the hot towels down on the couch between Sam and Michael. They quickly folded them while I moved the sheets to the dryer and started a load of Michael's clothes.

And so our days progressed. Sam and I were closer than ever, and Michael was like our child that we took care of and had fun with in the water. It was easy to fall into this pattern of fucking, swimming, and housekeeping, but I told myself that I had to gird myself against it. It was a dangerous path, when I could see the end of it in less than a week. I didn't want it to end, but I could see no way around it. Telling myself to just enjoy the time that Sam and I had together, I was able to dispel the negative thoughts of the future and be in the moment with him, at least for a while.

CHAPTER FOURTEEN

On Wednesday, I had planned a big meal for dinner and made sure Sam had invited his dad and uncle. They were due in at six, and Michael and Sam helped me by setting the table and making a salad. Michael was very sad about having to go home, and Sam was unusually distracted, even nervous. I wanted to know what that was about, but we didn't have time to talk privately.

Michael was all packed and brought his suitcase down to the great room. The beach house had had a good cleaning while we were at the beach, thanks to a service I had hired for that morning. Michael had turned on lights that showed this great house in its best light. The country-style steak had been cooking all afternoon, so the house smelled strongly of it.

Then the knock on the front door came. Michael bounded over to answer it. Cam came in with a tall thick man who I assumed was Uncle Dale. He had lost most of his hair but had shaved it short so that it wasn't as noticeable. He was average-looking, but he seemed to have a permanent frown on his face.

"Michael, my boy. How are you? Did you have fun?" Cam asked.

"It was great, dad. Brand took good care of us."

Cam turned to me and shook my hand. "Brand, thanks so much for letting the boys stay with you and extending their vacation."

"It was my pleasure, Cam."

"I bet it was," Uncle Dale said under his breath.

Cam looked disgusted. "Brand, this is my brother, Dale."

"Nice to meet you, Dale." He didn't extend his hand, so neither did I.

"So you're the one that my nephew has taken up with?" Dale asked, with a tone to his voice that wasn't pleasant.

I could see that he was choosing to look at Sam while talking to me. I looked at Sam for help. Sam stepped in, like the gallant white knight I knew him to be, "Uncle Dale, if you have a problem, it's with me."

"You are just doing what any red-blooded man would do in your position. We are NOMARs, and we fuck. That is what we do." This time he looked directly at me as he talked.

"Dale, please!" Cam yelled. "Michael."

Dale did look chagrined for a second as he glanced at Michael. "All right, I'll keep my opinions to myself."

"Dinner's ready. Let's sit down and eat," Sam said in his commanding voice. I had never heard him use it before in public, so it immediately turned me on. My body responded to it, even as I told myself to stop.

We ate dinner, and it seemed to soften everyone up. There was complete silence at first until Michael started to tell his dad about our last five days. Cam seemed fascinated that we had para-sailed and asked a lot of questions about it. They all complimented me on my cooking, even Dale.

At the end of dinner, I had made an apple pie, and that was what finally melted the ice.

"He might be a keeper, Sam," Dale said under his breath to his nephew as he ate a second piece of pie.

"Tell me about it. I think I might have gained ten pounds these past five days." Sam laughed as he rubbed his belly.

"So, Sam, you gonna stay with Brand until he leaves on Saturday?" Cam asked.

"If you don't need me back at work this week," Sam answered, with a hopeful note in his voice.

"No, we can make do without you this week, but we have a big project out at the Peterson's place next week."

"I'll be home for that."

"Make sure you are."

I recognized this for what it was. Cam knew he was fighting a losing battle with Sam over me, so he had conceded and was letting Sam have his fun, but making sure that he knew to rush back home afterwards.

We all rose from dinner, and Michael gave me a big hug saying, "Will we get to see you again, Brand?"

"I hope so," I told him. "But if not, you have my number and you can call anytime."

"Thanks so much for everything," Michael said as his eyes shifted quickly over to Sam. Michael could feel the bond between his older brother and me almost as well as we could.

"No problem." I shook hands with Cam and reluctantly and awkwardly with Dale as they left. We walked them down the steps and I was delighted to see Sam's truck parked in front of the house. I had just always assumed and pictured it as one of those big new Rams, but instead it was an old Ford with the side rails over the tires and the big cab.

"I love your truck," I said to him as we stood there.

"It's not new and the best, like you like."

"No, but that's what I like about it."

Sam flashed a huge smile and we waved goodbye to his family until they were gone into the darkening night.

"Well, that went better than I expected," Sam said as we ascended the stairs.

"Really?"

"Yeah. Dale can be an asshole when he wants to be. I'm pretty sure that's why dad brought him down here tonight."

"He's just saying what a lot of people are thinking. It's one thing that you will have to deal with for the next few days if we're going to go out."

"I'm okay with that." He chuckled as he put me in a headlock and dragged me through the front door. "Now, I've been wanting to fuck you in one of those rocking chairs on the porch ever since that day I was watching you as you sat there waiting for me."

"Oh, you have, have you?"

He stopped and stammered a little, "I—I mean if you want to."

"Of course I do, you big lug. I'll go get a bottle of lube. Why don't you turn all of these lights off? We can just use the moonlight, can't we?"

"Yeah." Sam grinned at me. I was up the stairs and back down in a heartbeat. Sam had darkened the house, and I poured us two glasses of wine and carried them out to the porch, where he was already rocking.

"This really has been a magical week," he said, waxing poetic as he looked at the moon and the ocean.

"It's about to get better." I smirked as I dropped my clothes on the porch planks and knelt in front of my stud. He put his weight on his elbows on the arms of the rocker so that I could yank his pants off. He wasn't wearing underwear, and when I looked up, he burst out laughing.

"I guess I need to do some laundry." He yanked his shirt off in one quick movement and pulled me onto his lap. I draped myself over him, and he gently rocked us while we looked out at the beautiful and eerie landscape. Occasionally we could hear people walking by on the beach, but we were mostly alone.

I could feel his big cock growing under me and used my ass to gently graze it, feeling him respond. I slid out of his lap and twisted to the ground, coming face to face with his cock. Licking and sucking his balls first, I moved up to his hard cock and coated it in a generous layer of slobber as Sam rocked. I couldn't wait to get that big monster inside me again.

Sam was slick enough from my saliva, so I just lubed my ass before I climbed up onto the chair. I was facing him and he helped me put my legs over the arms and settle into his lap. I held onto the wooden balls at the top of the chair as he found my asshole with the tip of his cock and punched it through. He immediately filled me up with that feeling that I was part of him, connected to him.

"Push it all the way in, Master." I moaned.

Sam let a groan escape his throat when I used his title. He looked into my eyes in the pale light—I know he saw that I needed him as much as he needed me. He kept feeding me cock until he was all in and I was sitting on his nest of pubic hair as it tickled my ass cheeks.

"Fuck, Master." I groaned.

"Put your arms on my neck or shoulders," he commanded.

I complied and he begun to rock us, his gaze never leaving mine. The rocking motion was unique, and I loved the way it made me feel, like his cock was pumping into me and then back out, even though I wasn't sure that it really was.

"Oh, God, Master, I wouldn't wish to be anywhere else in the world but right here."

He responded by moving his hands to my lower back and hips and saying, "Let go of me and lean back." I trusted him implicitly and followed his commands. Now I was leaning back into space above the porch and he was rocking back and forth, drilling into me deeper and deeper, his big cock punching my prostate over and over, sending waves of pleasure right to my brain stem.

Sam fucked with a faster pace and soon was on the verge of his climax.

"Let me taste it, Master," I pleaded.

"Very well," he said, lifting me up off his cock and onto the porch. I knelt and sucked his fiery sword into my mouth just as he blasted his climax right down my throat. I sucked his delicious seed until he had stopped dribbling it and then I cleaned his shaft.

"You are one hot little fucker," he told me, breathing heavily.

"Thank you, Master, but you are the hot one. I am just basking in your heat."

"I'll give you basking . . ." His big paws were on me, pulling me up and spinning me around. "Grab the railing," he directed.

Sam pushed my feet together and re-inserted his sea serpent into its dark cave. I felt like my legs might give out from his command of me, but I felt in my heart that he would catch me if they did.

I knew I was tighter than ever in this position and it felt like he was literally stabbing me with that hot cock as he slid it into me. "Aw, fuck, Master." I moaned.

Once he hit bottom, Sam began to rock back and forth in the rocking chair, first pulling his cock out and then driving it back home again. It was a genius piece of fucking, and I gave him creativity points on top of the points he was already earning for dominating me and fucking destroying my ass.

I grunted as I tried to hang onto the railing, my breathing becoming shallow and harsh. Sam was making small noises of pleasure as well, and his breathing was quicker than normal. He was reaching forward on each in-stroke, pinching my nipples just to add another level of pleasure onto this fuck.

As Sam approached his climax, he leaned forward, picked me up and pulled me back onto his chest. I laid my head back onto his broad shoulder, and his big hands held my ass above his crotch, giving him the ultimate angle to fuck up into me as hard and fast as he could. He destroyed my little puckered hole until he fell over the cliff of his climax and sprayed the inside of my ass with his sweet hot cum.

"Fuck! You are bringing something out of me that I never

knew I had," he said, breathlessly. He rubbed my chest with his big rough hands.

"I knew you had it in there." I straightened up, and his cock popped out of my ass, leaving me with that incredible empty feeling that I hated so much. "I love your creativity, your stamina, your silent dominance, your concern for me, and mostly your love of the fuck."

I sat back down on his lap, facing him, and wiped the sweat off his brow and into his hair. "Master, what will we do now that we can fuck anywhere and as often as we like?"

"I guess we will fuck everywhere and as often as possible. You okay with that?"

"Yes, sir," I said, excitement shading my voice.

"You tired?"

"Yes, sir."

"Let's go to bed then. We have two full days of fun ahead of us."

"Yes, we do." I laughed and stood up, helping him out of the rocking chair and into the house.

The next night I made reservations at Benny Rappa's, which was a really good Italian restaurant in a tiny mobile home on Highway 17. It was small and romantic, and I wondered how Sam would handle it.

We received a lot of attention as we made our way to our table for two behind the hostess. Not many of the patrons had ever seen a guy as big as Sam, and the fact that he was with a marked guy who was probably his Servant was almost more than they could take. They excitedly whispered to each other, asking if he was a famous athlete.

We ordered and I asked him, "You okay with this?"

"With what? The attention?"

"Yeah."

"It's a little out of my comfort zone, but I'm getting better at handling it, aren't I?"

"Yes, you are. It's different than being with Michael, though, so I would understand if you don't like it."

"I like you, so it will have to do." His voice was flat.

"I like you, too."

"Yeah, we need to talk about that."

"Here?" I asked him, surprised.

"Sure, why not?"

"Okay." I could only guess that this setting, with other people nearby, helped him be able to talk about this sensitive subject.

"You know I have to go back to work next week. What are your plans?"

"I'm going to go visit my family for a few days before heading to Pittsburgh." I ventured out on the limb. "Or, I could visit my family and then come visit you."

He swallowed hard and said, "You know I would love that, but I think you need to see what it's like being out of The Service. I think you should go home for a while, date other people, fuck a lot of guys, and see what it's like on your own."

I could see that this was hard for him to say. "Why?" I asked, mortally wounded.

"Well, because I think we had our fun and now I need to go back to the real world and you to your glamorous rich life."

"But is that what you want?"

"It doesn't matter what I want. I'm just a regular guy working construction, and you are like something sent down from heaven and . . . regular guys don't get those kind of presents."

"It *does* matter. We have to make our decision together."

Our food came and we started to eat. Sam continued after several bites. "What would you do . . . come to live in little Lake View and be bored out of your mind waiting for me to come home each day?"

"If that's what we want to do, then I'll do it."

Sam looked at me with his poker face on. "I'm not going to have you miserable and hating me for it—blaming me for dragging you down."

I swallowed my spaghetti and said quietly, "What if that is enough for me and what I want?"

"Is it?"

I couldn't be anything but honest with him. "No."

"I knew it." He looked down into his plate of raviolis like he might be sick.

"But maybe *you* want more. You could come with me." I was hopeful that this last-ditch effort would work.

"And leave my dad and not help Michael? I'm just a construction worker who caught the eye of a really hot marked guy on vacation. You take me out of that, and I'm just a non-educated, non-travelled hick."

"You're *my* hick," I said, feeling my eyes tearing up.

"And you're my light, at least for the next few days. We will keep in touch and maybe spend our vacation together next summer, if you haven't moved on by then." Sam said this with finality, and I knew it was for the better to just let it drop, at least for now. I knew this had been coming, but I was still heartbroken about it.

We had come to Benny Rappa's in Sam's old truck and now rode back to the beach house in it. When he pulled in and parked, I knew that I needed him inside me in order to feel better. I reached over and unzipped his cargo shorts. He looked down at first and then over to my face. My eyes were misty, and he reached out and put one big hand around the scruff of my neck and squeezed it.

I pulled his big cock out of his fly and bent over to suck it into my mouth. He spread his legs, unbuttoned the top of his pants, and guided my head down onto his flesh root with one big hand. I loved his cock in my mouth and I only wished that

I could swallow the whole thing. He tasted delicious and I sucked him until he was rock-hard and ready to fuck.

Sam gently put his hands under my arms and pulled me over onto his lap. I had taken my shorts off while I was sucking him, and now my ass was open for business. I slid down on his big pole, loving the feeling of his cock filling me up and I tracked his progress as gravity pulled me down onto his lap.

When he was buried up to the nuts in me, Sam held me there and used his big thumbs to wipe the tears away from my cheeks. "This is better, isn't it?"

"Yes, Master."

Sam slow-fucked me right there and then turned me around, bent me over the big old-fashioned steering wheel, and fucked me again. I felt much better afterwards, and we laughed as we tried to find our clothes and get redressed to walk ten feet to the beach house.

Friday was our last full day together, and Sam and I made a pact to make the most of it. We started the day with a hard fucking and moved on to riding the waves together and then sitting in the edge of the water in our chairs. I loved that we were at the point where we were comfortable either talking or just sitting and reading together. Sam and I had a lot in common, besides the sex, and I enjoyed telling him about the things I was reading about and listening to what he found interesting.

For lunch, I made BLTs, and Sam and I spent an hour or so fucking on the couch and in the armchair before taking a nap together, me wrapped in his arms as we stretched naked on the couch under a blanket.

Waking up an hour later, we went back to the ocean for the last time and body-surfed for several hours. Sam let me sit on his lap while we floated in the deep water and I wrapped my legs around him. We talked about next summer and how we would keep in touch. By the time we were finished talking, the sun was setting, and we headed inside.

"I really love the beach," Sam said, looking out onto the ocean.

"Me, too," I agreed. "Especially now," I said, looking at him.

He smiled, and we went inside to get ready for dinner. Sam was taking me out for Japanese. He was insistent on paying, and we enjoyed the tableside hibachi show that the chef put on, as well as the food.

"Well, thank you for dinner, Sam," I said as we walked back to the car, smelling like oil and fried rice.

"I have a feeling I will be getting paid back for it in spades tonight."

"I think that is a pretty safe bet," I said lustily. I let Sam drive and we headed home.

CHAPTER FIFTEEN

"Do you think you will miss me, Master?"

"More than you will miss me."

"What do you mean?"

"I mean I will always remember this. It has been the most fantastic experience of my life these two weeks, but for you, this is just your life and it will fade into all of the other experiences that you will have until you barely remember me, let alone miss me."

"That is not true," I said firmly. "I also have had a fantastic experience, and when we part tomorrow, it will be a deep pain for me that may never heal."

"I didn't know that's how you felt."

We had pulled into the driveway. "If you would come with me, I would be perfectly happy for the rest of my life." It cost me to be so vulnerable and so honest. I felt like I was flayed open, exposed to the world. "You would never have to work again, and we could go wherever you like whenever we want."

He got out of the car, joined me in front of it, and said, "I probably would be perfectly happy also." We headed up the stairs. "I'll tell you what. Maybe we can consider some type of compromise."

Now I was interested. I could feel my heart start to beat faster with just that glimmer of hope that he might come with me. "Like what?"

"Well, our business slows in the winter, so maybe you and I could hang out then."

It wasn't what I was hoping for, but it was something to consider. "That's an idea. I am used to seeing a lot of white stuff in the winter," I said dryly.

"I have plenty of white stuff for you," he said, laughing as he pushed me through the door into the house. "What do you want to do on our last night?"

"I don't care, as long as your cock is buried inside me."

"Sounds perfect to me."

"Can you build a fire?" I asked.

"Sure," Sam said as he looked at the stone fireplace. I had seen all of the materials for fire-making there in the tinder box, so I knew he had everything he needed. I started moving the furniture back from in front of the fireplace, clearing a large area.

"You worried I might set the place on fire?" he smirked.

"No, sir. I have other things in mind."

He raised his eyebrows, showing his interest. I walked over to the thermostat and turned the air way down so that it would be freezing inside the house. Then I walked into the downstairs bedroom and grabbed the blankets, sheets and pillows off the bed and carried them into the great room, dropping them on the couch.

Sam had a good start on the fire, and I loved the light it gave off. I closed the drapes in the great room and turned some of the lights out. Walking back to the bedroom, I hefted the Queen-size mattress off the bed and folded it in half. I struggled with getting it through the door frame for a while before looking up and seeing Sam there smiling at me.

"Well, are you going to help me or not?" I asked.

"I kinda like seeing you struggle . . ."

"Ass," I said, tongue-in-cheek.

"Okay, okay," he said, laughing and pulling the mattress.

We maneuvered it into the great room, set it on the floor, and I went to turn off the rest of the lights.

"This is pretty cool," Sam said to me, his face illuminated by the fire light.

"I have one more surprise for you on our last night."

"Really?"

"Be right back," I said mysteriously.

Walking back to the bedroom, I reached up in the closet and retrieved a box that had come for me earlier in the week. I had hidden it there, since I knew that Michael and Sam weren't likely to use this room. After our para-sailing experience, Sam had mentioned that he was turned on by me in a harness, so I had jumped on the internet and overnighted some equipment to the beach house.

I tore into the box and pulled out a set of leather cuffs—two for the wrists and two for the ankles. Each cuff had a mini-carabiner clip attached to it. I put them on, and they fit perfectly.

Next out of the box were a set of bungee cords and straps. Finally, the last and biggest thing in the box was a full leather harness for me to wear. I smiled to myself, thinking of what the look on Sam's face was going to be when I walked out there wearing this.

I strapped on the collar, put on the cross breastplate, put on the cock strap, and lastly put on the leather belt. I hooked everything together, surprised at how well it fit. I didn't even have to adjust any of the straps to fit me.

"You okay in there?" Sam yelled.

"I'm great! You ready for your surprise?"

"Ready."

I felt a little foolish, but I grabbed the bungees and headed out. Sam was lying on the mattress in front of the fire, completely naked. In this light, his skin looked even darker, and every muscle was outlined. Sam was stunning and he stopped me in my tracks as I came around the sofa.

He had a huge grin on his face—until he saw me and his

brain registered what he was seeing. The smile vanished and his poker face was back, only this time I could see the lust in his eyes. He rose up on his knees and just stared at me. I turned slowly so that he could see all of me. When I turned back around, Sam was licking his chops.

Sam jumped to his feet, grabbed the O ring on my chest and pulled me onto the mattress. I started to ask him what he thought, but he closed my mouth by pushing my chin up and softly placing his index finger on my lips. He whirled me around and pressed on the back of my knees. He grabbed the leather straps on my back and lowered me onto all fours. I heard the familiar sound of him jacking his cock with lube and then unexpectedly, I felt his big fingers on my hole and then sliding inside. The cool lube on his fingers slicked my hole while he worked his fingers inside me.

Moaning, I showed him my pleasure.

"Quiet," he warned.

I was immediately set on fire. I loved nothing more than Sam going into Master-mode and dominating me. I bit my bottom lip to keep from grunting and was rewarded by Sam replacing his fingers with his big manhood. He pushed his cockhead inside me and then gripped the leather straps of my harness, pulling me back onto him the rest of the way.

Sam was able to fill me up like no one I had ever fucked with before, and I was so hot for him. By the time he buried himself in me to his nuts, I was sweating from the fire and ready to be fucking drilled. He nestled up beside my hips, grabbed the straps on my back with both hands and then started to fucking tear me up.

Sam destroyed my ass, using the harness to do it, and came faster than he ever had before. I hoped that meant that he was as hot as I was. He continued to rock me back and forth through his climax, growling through his clenched teeth as he filled me up with his hot cum.

"God damn." Sam groaned as he collapsed on top of me, knocking me to the mattress and the air out of my lungs. He continued to mini-thrust into me as he lay on top of me and curled his fingers into mine.

"Master, you constantly impress me," I said, after regaining my ability to talk.

Sam pulled out of me, then flipped me over under him as he hovered above me. He was looking down into my eyes and said, "You're the one who walked out here in that getup, knowing what it was going to do to me."

"And you didn't even have to use the ball gag I bought."

We both laughed and Sam said, "Where did you get all of this stuff?"

"When you had such a painful hard-on the other day and blamed it on the sight of me in the para-sailing harness, I ordered it and had it overnighted to the beach house."

"You sneaky little bastard."

"Well, did you like it or not?"

"Couldn't you tell?"

"I could, actually, but the fun is just starting." I reached over to the bag of bungee cords and retrieved a rubber cord.

"What's that?"

"You'll see, Master. Can you help me get it set up?" He sat up on his knees and I unfolded the rubber cord and said, "We need it to go around the mattress." I saw the quizzical look on his face and almost laughed. It was a tight fit, but we eventually got it on the sides of the mattress.

"What the fuck is this?" Sam asked.

I smiled at him as he tried to figure out what he was looking at. Sam fingered the rubber cording and noticed that metal circles were embedded in it every foot or so. I pulled a bungee cord out of the bag, hooked it into one of the circles on the side of the mattress and then hooked the other end onto my wrist. I watched Sam's face as I hooked it in.

His eyes were literally popping and he was constantly licking his lips. "Oh, this could be fun!" He unbuckled me and then buckled me back to see how it worked. "You're going to be in such trouble now, Brand."

"That's what I was hoping for, Master."

Sam put a big hand on my chest and pushed me onto my back. He had a serious look on his face as he connected my wrists to the corners of the mattress. Then he moved down and connected my ankles to the other corners so that I was spread-eagled, harnessed, and completely open to him. He moved around me and ended up above my head, feeding his sloppy cock down into my mouth for me to clean up for him, which I did, gladly.

When he pulled his cock out of my mouth, I was left like a baby bird, still hungry for more. Sam walked back around me and put his hand on his chin, considering. I guess he had figured out that while this position was great for blowjobs and dominating someone, it wasn't so hot for fucking. But the beauty of this set-up was that Sam could change my position at any time.

And he did. With a sly smile on his face and a twinkle in his eyes, he unhooked my ankles and bent my legs at the knee. He re-hooked my ankles with the bungees and suddenly I was in the perfect position. One side of Sam's mouth turned up into a smile and he sidled up to my upturned ass. In this position, the bottoms of my feet were flat on his stomach and my ass was completely flush with his crotch.

"Fuck me, Master," I whined.

"Don't make me get that ball gag," he said with a hint of warning to his voice.

I closed my mouth and tried not to make any noise as he inserted his saliva-covered cock back inside me. I was unable to move most of my body, but I could arch my back, which I did as he filled me up with more man-meat than I could handle. His cock seemed bigger than ever and when I finally felt his pubic hairs tickling my ass cheeks, I knew I was as full of cock as I would ever get. And even though I knew I should have been sad about this coming to an end, at the moment I couldn't feel anything but pure joy and pleasure.

Sam seemed to like the harness and strap system. He gave me a good hard fucking, eventually crawling over me on all fours and finishing us off. We came at almost the same time, his abs rubbing my cock until I exploded onto both of our chests.

"What the fuck are you doing to me?" Sam asked me as he stared down at me.

"I hope I am making you happy, Master."

"You are definitely making me the happiest I have ever been, but I have never had any experience like this in my life. I have never fucked like this, I have never known anyone like you, and I have never felt this way before."

"Good. My plan is working." I smirked.

"Oh, you have a plan, do you? What is it?"

"Fuck you so good that you won't leave me." I instantly blushed as I said it, feeling the heat in my ears and on my neck, as well as my face.

"It's a good plan. I like it," Sam said, encouraging me.

"Wanna go one more time, Master?"

"At least!"

Sam unhooked my legs, put some more logs on the fire, and held my drink up to my lips as he tilted my head forward. "You okay?" he checked with me.

"Yes, Master."

"Good." He re-hooked my legs to the corners again. I was a little surprised, because I thought he had seen that this position wasn't the best. Sam further surprised me by hooking bungee cords between my wrists and the corners and between my ankles and the corners—doubling the size of the previous restraints. I didn't know what he was planning but I sure loved that he was exploring this new sexual fetish with me.

"How's that?" Sam asked me.

"Good, Master, but now I can move around a lot more," I said with a raised eyebrow.

"Not for long." Sam smirked.

My throat was suddenly dry and I was left wondering what he had in store for me. Sam walked around to my head and sat down on the part of the mattress that was right above my head. Then I felt his big legs go under my arms and down the side of my torso. My head was now on his crotch and I felt the heat from his big cock as it touched my ear and cheek. I could not figure out what position he was going for.

And then it hit me like a ton of bricks. Sam slid down under me again—now my head was resting on his abs. He had put the bungee cords on my wrists and ankles so that I could more easily be moved up into the air. He slid down again and now my head rested on his big chest and his hot cock was under my lower back. With one more big push, he was in the sweet spot. His cock was directly under my asshole, and my head was resting on his shoulder.

Sam tried out the bungee cords to see how high he could lift me by pushing my hips up. I guess he liked what he saw, because he grunted his satisfaction. The higher he lifted me in the air, the tighter the restraints became, and at the apex of the lift, I was completely stretched out like a starfish.

Rubbing my cheek with his bearded face, Sam found my ear and whispered, "Stay quiet now, little one."

"Yes, sir," I croaked, feeling like I might explode just from hearing that one sentence from him.

Sam growled in my ear to show me that he didn't even want me to say that. I had thought that the quiet fucks were originally meant to hide our fucking from Sam's father, then to not arouse the suspicions of his brother, but now that they were all gone we were still doing it. Maybe Sam found it fucking hot, just like I did.

With some re-adjustment, Sam was finally able to snake his big python up into me. I strained against the restraints as his big cock stretched out my asshole and pushed my crotch higher into the air than the rest of my body. With a sudden switch from lifting my ass cheeks up, Sam moved his hands to the hollows in front of my hips and pulled me down, impaling me on his thick flagpole. It was painful and fantastic at the same time. If I wasn't on a gag order from him, I probably would have screamed. As it was, I bit my lip and squeezed my eyes shut.

I was now resting completely on top of him, but still pulled tight by the cords. I could feel every contour of his well-muscled body under me and his body heat, warmed by the fire. My sweat ran down my body and mixed with Sam's. He ran his hands lightly all over my body, pinching my nipples and jacking my semi-hard cock. Sam was able to send me to levels of pleasure that I had never known before and in that moment my whole being belonged to him.

Sam began to pump his hips under me, lifting me off him and then pulling me back down. I was completely helpless and at his mercy, thank God. He was dominating me like he had never done before. His big cock was destroying me from below and he relentlessly moved me up and down on top of him. He was churning his previous load of cum into butter that was being fucked right out of me as he pistoned back and forth inside me.

"Fuck." I groaned, unable to stay silent anymore. Sam's fucking slowed for just a second, and then he clamped one of his big hands over my mouth as he resumed the destruction of my ass. I bit the skin of one of his thick fingers gently as he thrust me up and down so quickly on his manhood. My asshole was sore and stretched wide as he moved it rapidly up his shaft and then back down.

His hand tasted salty on my lips and mouth. His cock felt like a hot knife inside me. His hand on my hip felt as permanent as a set of handcuffs. His chest felt like a hard mattress for my sore body. But above all, his stubbly cheek on my mine was the part of his body that was sending me over the edge. Sam's cheek barely touched me, but when it did, it sent electric shivers down my spine and straight into my cock.

I felt Sam's climax building, just like mine. The relentless pounding of my ass continued as I approached the cliff's edge and then fell over. I shot ropy strands of spunk on my new leather harness, and my ass muscles clamped shut in response.

"Oh, fuck." Sam growled into my ear as I squeezed him relentlessly. He buried deep in me and dropped another load of hot cum inside me.

Sam unhooked me from the restraints, and we lay together the rest of the night, spooning in front of the fire, his cock firmly planted inside me.

Chapter Sixteen

Saturday morning was so painful for me that I didn't think I would be able to stand it. Seeing Sam pack his bags and load his truck was one of the most excruciating experiences of my life. I wanted to stay in bed all morning fucking, but Sam was smarter than me. He knew that would just make it harder.

"Sam," I started the conversation, but didn't know how to say it.

"Yes," he offered, equally warring with his emotions.

"I don't know how to say it or what to say."

He held his arms out to me, wide open. I went to him and rested my head on his chest. "I know."

I felt my heart in my throat. "Would it help if I begged you?"

"No, and it would probably turn me on . . ."

I breathed in deeply of his smell, telling myself to remember everything about him.

"Would it help if I tried to restrain you?"

"Maybe. I'm almost to that point," I said.

Suddenly there was a tone of hope to his voice, "You would consider coming to live in Lake View?"

"Maybe, if I got to see you."

He squeezed me harder to his chest with his big arms and laughed. "You would completely freak out in Lake View, and they wouldn't know what to do with you."

"You could leave me harnessed to the bed, chained and spread-eagled. I wouldn't care."

142

"Don't tempt me." Sam's voice smoldered. He let go of me and pushed me back so he could see my face. "I know that you will enjoy seeing your family today."

"It's been a while. Tell Michael and Cam that I said hi," I said as I walked him down the steps and to his truck.

"Don't be sad. I will talk to you soon, and we will make plans for winter," Sam said, his deep voice soothing me, even if his words did not. "Thank you, Brand, for the best two weeks, including last night."

I smiled and said, "It was pretty fucking spectacular, wasn't it?"

Sam got into the truck and closed the door. "It was the most spectacular night of my life."

I grabbed his arm on the window frame and said, "Thanks, Sam, for everything."

He nodded and grinned at me as he drove off, my heart shattering into a million pieces as I stood and waved. I quickly turned and walked up the stairs so that no one could see my pain.

My visit with my dad and my brothers was nice, but I was in a really crappy mood. I hadn't seen them in close to a year, and they had not changed much in that time. I took them to dinner several times, buying my father a new riding lawn mower and my brother a car. I could tell that they had missed me, but I was a different person now than even a month ago. I was really missing Sam, and I knew that I didn't fit in with the people of my family or my hometown anymore. I decided right then to go to Pittsburgh. It was where I had wanted to live after graduating from the SA. I had some friends that had relocated there after their time in the SA and others that relocated there after their Service.

The days seemed to drag by and the only bright spots for me were when I would get a text from Sam or Michael. I guess

Sam could hear the despondency in my texts or he was feeling the same way, based on his texts.

You need to buck up and get on with your life. I know it is difficult, but this is a new beginning for u and u should enjoy it. I would not know this man that is so sad.

I took Sam's text to heart and vowed to start the day fresh as I drove my rental to the airport. The flight to Pittsburgh was short and hardly worth the first-class fare, but I was determined to start this new adventure on the right foot. I had called Patrick from the airport. He had more good news about our investments, as usual, and I filled him in on all of my happenings since the last time we had talked. I concealed the fact that I was in love with Sam, not wanting to hurt Patrick's feelings. He told me that he was going to come visit me when I got settled, if it was okay with me, which it was.

I had asked permission to use Patrick's real estate broker, Eric, and he had given his information to me. Eric had rented me an eighty-year-old house on the West side of Pittsburgh and had it furnished. I had the address and rented a car from the airport and drove to it. It was a good house with character, and Eric had gotten someone to purchase a lot of the essentials for me to get me started like sheets, towels, cleaning supplies, toilet paper, and some simple groceries. He also had the satellite TV installed, as well as the electrical, gas, and internet turned on.

I settled into the house, unpacking my clothes from my suitcase and locating the nearest grocery store on my iPhone. I went grocery shopping and made myself a nice dinner afterwards. It was really quiet in the house, but it was nice after the noise of the beach. I was excited about exploring the city tomorrow.

The next morning, I went out shopping and exploring. I wasn't sure this was where I was going to put down roots, so I really didn't want to buy anything permanent, like furniture. I picked up a few things that I wanted and had lunch while I was out. I loved going through the Fort Pitt tunnel under Mount Washington, seeing nothing but mountain, and then coming out of it, suspended on a bridge at the confluence of three major rivers and seeing all of downtown Pittsburgh right in front of me. It was a spectacular view, and I was energized by it. I took pictures and sent them to Sam and Michael, asking them each to come and visit.

I already liked the Steelers, but it was baseball season, so I bought a Pirates jersey in the Strip so I would fit in with everyone else. By the time I got back home, I was dripping in sweat from the heat, and I took a long cool shower to feel more like myself. I noticed in the shower that I was putting on some weight, so I made a mental note to hire a personal trainer tomorrow. Laughing to myself that my body was missing Sam's workouts as much as my heart was, I dried off and turned on the TV.

It was the Pirates pre-game show, and I realized that they would be on in a few minutes and that it was Friday night. Not wanting to watch it by myself, I got dressed, including my new jersey, and headed to a local bar I had seen on the way from the airport called The Bar at the Tonidale. It was an intriguing name for a bar, and even though I had no clue what The Tonidale was, I gave it a shot. It was a little dive bar that had one big room filled with booths and tables that opened onto a half-rectangular bar with a side area for pool.

I was surprised how many guys were there. It must have been the place to go after work on Fridays. The very first booth was empty, and it faced a big plasma-screen TV on the wall, so I took a seat. Of course, when I had entered, a lot of the patrons had turned to see who it was, and I got several shocked expressions from those on the barstools. I didn't look at the guys seated near me, instead scrambling to take my seat and see the game.

The Pirates had already scored on an Alvarez home run in

the first inning and were up 1-0. The waiter came by my table, took a look at my mark, and froze for a second. He finally asked me what I was drinking, and I ordered a Corona Lite with a lime.

I loved watching a game while at a bar. There was something about the conversations, discussions, and the cheers that really made the sporting event even more exciting to me. Once while travelling, Patrick and I had gone to a bar to watch a football game and a marked guy had come in trolling. It was fascinating to watch him. He walked from booth to booth, from table to table, from barstool to barstool. He evaluated each and every man in the bar. When he saw me and then looked at Patrick, he mouthed the word *Service* and I nodded, even though I thought this was rude. When the marked guy had completely made his rounds and evaluated every man in the place, he walked over to one of the guys on the barstools and whispered something to him. The guy stood up, grinning, and they left together, the marked guy winking at me on the way out. Patrick had commented to me what a dangerous game that was for him, and I had agreed. I could never see myself doing that.

This bar was especially energized, and it wasn't long before I had a suitor.

"Hey, whattsup?"

A cunning linguist, I see. "What do you want?" Patrick had taught me how to defend myself, and the first step was to be blunt.

He was a decent-looking guy. Average height, but nice biceps from working out. He was bald, but probably a red-head, judging by his skin tone. He was a little drunk, but not sloppy. "Just wanted to see if you wanted to watch the game."

"I am watching the game." This drew a chorus of laughter and raspberries from the crowd, who had stopped watching the game and was eagerly invested in watching this guy's plight for their own entertainment.

"No, I mean with me."

"No, thanks, dude. I'm good."

He hadn't prepared for this outcome, and now he didn't know what to do next. "You sure?"

"I'm positive." I saw his face drop and he headed back to the bar, shaking his head. I turned right back to the TV, not wanting to antagonize anyone or make him feel any worse than he was for getting shot down.

The next inning brought the next suitor. This time he was a short Italian-looking guy with big biceps and a well-defined chest. *Did all the guys in this town have those guns?* He came bearing a gift of another Corona Lite, which I didn't take, but he did score a point for at least being observant enough to know what I was drinking.

"You up for some company tonight?" he asked, a little too slickly.

I repeated my line from earlier. "No, thanks, I'm good."

"Come on, man. You gotta give me just a little bit of something something." With this elegant phrase, he grabbed his crotch, just in case I didn't get his drift.

"Yeah, that's not happening," I said plainly.

"What's your problem?" His voice had gotten louder and meaner. This was turning into a problem, and I probably was going to have to leave.

"Dude, he said no, now move on." A deep voice that was firm and authoritative spoke from behind my short Italian. The voice was connected to a very tall, magnificent piece of man. He turned to the bar patrons and said, "Guys, he's in here to watch the game just like us. He doesn't want to be harassed by you jag-offs. If he wants to fuck with one of you, he will let you know. Until then, leave him the hell alone."

"Thanks," I said to him. I wondered whether it was just him being helpful or whether it was a brilliant move to get my attention.

"No, problem." He was blond with a buzz cut in a military style. He had huge biceps that wouldn't even fit under his shirt sleeves. On one arm was a giant tattoo of a cross. He was really cute and at least six-foot-five, wearing a dress shirt, jeans, and flip-flops. I couldn't help but look down at his feet while he was standing beside my booth. They were big, masculine, and beautiful.

"I'm Ian. I'm sitting with my buddies right over there at that table." He pointed. "If you really want some company, come sit with us. It will keep the riff-raff away from you."

"I'm Brand. I think I'll be good for now, thanks to you."

"Okay, cool." Ian turned and walked back to his table. I watched him go, noticing that he had a great ass. His two friends seemed nice enough, as well. One of them was drop-dead hot with black hair and a thick body. The other was bald and on the skinny side, but still hot. I wondered how these three really good-looking men were friends.

I turned back to the game, smiling to myself because I suddenly felt a lot better, but at the same time feeling guilty, thinking of Sam. I was able to get through two innings before the next drunk guy, and I do mean *drunk*, came over and sat down at my booth. He was sloppy drunk and couldn't even string together a complete sentence.

I glanced over at Ian's table. The three guys were all smiling and Ian raised his shoulders and pointed at the empty chair.

I got up, leaving the drunk in the booth, and made my way over to their table. They all were laughing and high-fiving me as I took my seat.

"Brand, this is Jordy," Ian said, indicating the dark-haired friend. "And this is Jay."

"Hey guys. I'm glad that I could be your entertainment tonight, since the game is not that exciting."

They laughed, and we talked about all the freaks in the bar tonight. I liked all three guys—they seemed to be nice and were friends from school. They were curious about me, of course, and why I had decided to come to Pittsburgh after The Service. They had a lot of questions and we laughed and drank while I answered them. The Pirates won, so everyone was in a good mood.

"Well, guys, I'm gonna head home. You guys wanna come over and watch the game at my house on Sunday?"

"Sure," they all said excitedly.

"Cool. Here's my cell phone number." I handed my card to Ian. "Text me and I'll send you the address."

"Awesome," Ian said, studying the card. I could almost see his brain working. I knew he wanted to go home with me tonight, I could just feel it, but he was able to control himself and said, "See ya."

"Bye." I left the bar alone, much to everyone's surprise but mine.

I went home and jacked off thinking about Ian and then called Sam, who didn't pick up, but overall, it had been a good night.

CHAPTER SEVENTEEN

The next day, I made a list of house stuff that I needed and I went to Home Depot to pick up some odds and ends. After Home Depot, I needed to make several more stops. I considered going to see a movie later.

I got the things I wanted in Home Depot and walked to the garden section outside. I did like being outdoors and gardening, which I had missed for the last six years. However, it was going to have to wait until I bought a house somewhere, because I was not going to all the effort and time for a rental property. I decided to buy two geraniums already in pots to put beside the front door. I was just picking the ones I wanted when I saw him.

He was obviously some type of construction worker, but he was dressed pretty strangely. He had a khaki shirt on with the sleeves torn off, short cargo shorts, and some type of motocross boots that went up to his knees. He was deeply tanned from the sun and was fucking ripped. His biceps weren't gigantic, but were so defined they looked cartoonish. He was average height and athletically thin with light brown hair that was cut short on the sides, but not the top.

He walked right by me on his way out of the garden center. He smiled at me and then saw the mark. I liked that in a guy—someone who was a nice person, even when there was no reason to be. I was a little disappointed to see him leave, but went ahead and got my plants and carried them to the register. I pulled a little wagon over and loaded it up with my purchases before heading to the car. While I was checking out,

I saw the construction worker getting a palette loaded onto a flatbed trailer.

I walked out to my car and started to load it. Afterwards, I was looking for the place to return the wagon, and I saw it beside where the flatbed was being loaded. I walked it over and saw my construction guy watching me. Rolling the wagon into the corral for it, I said to him, "What you buying?"

"Landscaping stones."

"Nice," I said, and went to turn to leave.

"You?"

I turned back, "Nothing special. I just moved into an old house and I need a lot of small stuff."

"What part of town?" he asked. He was engaging me without being desperate about it.

"West End."

"That's where I live, too. I'm Frank, but most people call me Crash." He flashed a huge grin at me.

"Really? Why?"

"I like to race things—cars, cycles, quads, you know. I used to crash a lot when I was learning how."

That explained the weird motocross boots. "That's a cool nickname, then." I laughed. "I'm Brand and new to town."

"Really? You want me to show you around sometime?"

"I'd like that. Here's my cell phone number." I handed him a card.

He took it with a rough hand that was, at least, clean. "Cool."

"Maybe early next week . . . like Monday night?" I decided.

"Sure. See ya." I watched him pocket my card and I waved as I turned away from him. Checking my phone, I saw that Ian had texted, asking for my address for tomorrow. My week was getting better and better.

At the house, I did some little things like hang some pictures and repair the front step that had a chip missing in it.

I liked being by myself, and the time passed rapidly. I ordered a pizza for dinner and ate it in front of the TV. Having just cleaned up and wondering what I might have for dessert, I was surprised by a knock on the front door. I hadn't been able to get the doorbell to work yet, even though I replaced the batteries.

I opened the door, and there was Ian.

"I hope you don't mind me coming over," he said and I heard the lust in his tone of voice. "I just found it hard to wait."

"Wait for what, Ian?" I decided to make him swing a little since he had stuck his neck out.

He looked stunned and then hung his head slightly. "I . . . just thought . . ." He went silent and looked down at me with pleading eyes.

"I'm just jagging you. Come on in," I finally said to him, opening the door wider.

Ian smiled and said, "Nice use of Pittsburghese."

"Thanks. I've been practicing." We walked into the living room and sat down. "You want a beer?"

"Yes, please. I kinda feel like a jackass now that I'm here."

"Why?"

"Well, you never said anything . . . and you didn't hint at anything . . ." He was completely unnerved.

I went and got us two beers and sat down on the couch with him. I kinda wanted to put him out of his misery, but I was enjoying seeing him squirm after he had just assumed that we were going to fuck.

"So you just assumed that we were going to fuck?" I kept my voice very serious.

He hung his head. "Yes."

"So did I," I said flatly.

He looked up quickly. "Really?"

"Yeah. Not today, though."

"I know. I got your text and then I put it in my GPS and then I found myself driving here and then walking up to the door."

I laughed.

He said, "I'll just come back tomorrow."

"Or you could stay and still come back tomorrow."

"Really?"

"Yeah." I finished my beer in one guzzle and walked over to him, straddling his long legs and sitting down on them. Ian's eyes widened and he was holding his breath. I grabbed the hem of his shirt and lifted it off over his head. His chest was very nice with a coating of blond hair, mostly on top and then trailing down into his jeans.

I took my time, rubbing his chest, pinching his nipples, and squeezing his biceps. Pulling my shirt off, I said, "You ever done this before, Ian?"

"Fuck?" he asked, almost laughing.

"Fuck a marked guy," I said bluntly.

"Oh. No. I've just fantasized about it some five million times or so."

"I'll try to live up to your fantasy, then." I smirked as I lowered myself to my knees and begun working on getting into his jeans. I pulled his flip-flops off and threw them in the corner and yanked his jeans off by the ankle cuffs. Ian raised himself up onto his arms to help me, giving me a great view of his hard biceps in action.

Ian was breathing rapidly as I pulled his boxers off and his semi-hard cock popped out. It was long and skinny, rising up out of a blond bush of hair that reminded me of Sam. The head was fat but had a definite bell-shape to it, like a tortoise shell.

Spreading his legs, I nestled between them and grabbed his cock by the root. My tongue flicked out and swiped his cockhead. Ian groaned and laid his head back. I began to lick his cock from the base to the head in giant swipes of my tongue. Once I had the whole thing wet, I sucked his knob into my mouth and felt him shake with a spasm of sensitivity.

I swallowed him completely down, making room for his cock to slightly enter my throat as I sucked him. I felt one big hand on the back of my head as he urged me on. Sucking with great force, I began to piston up and down on him, milking his big cock.

"God damn." He groaned just as I realized that he was about to come. Ian hadn't given any of the usual signals that he had reached his climax, so I was surprised.

I quickly pushed his cock as far into my mouth as I could and then felt him explode into his climax. His whole body shook with it and his hot semen hit me in the throat, filling my mouth up just as quickly as I could swallow. His cock juice was really tasty, so I didn't mind licking his cock clean of it.

Finally pulling off his cock, I sat back on my heels and looked up at Ian. He was smiling like a kid who had just faced a fear and jumped off a high dive platform. He started chuckling.

"Well, that was hot," I finally said to break the ice.

"Fucking terrific, that's what that was!" Ian exclaimed with energy.

"Wanna go again, or do you need time to reset?" God, I hoped he didn't need time. I needed to be fucked right now and fucked hard.

"I can go again."

"Excellent." I went to the bathroom and returned with a bottle of lube.

"Are we going to the bed?" he asked, innocently.

"Tomorrow, maybe." I smirked as I pulled the over-sized pillows off the sofa and threw them on the floor. I moved up onto the cushions on all fours next to him and said, "You gonna need a manual or what?"

We both burst out laughing and Ian kneeled on the couch

cushions behind me. I squirted lube into his hand and then my own. He slicked up his cock and I pushed two of my fingers inside my ass to lubricate myself. When Ian was ready, he nestled against my ass and fed his long cock inside me.

It was nothing like being fucked by Sam. Ian filled me length-wise, but he did not have the girth. He also did not have the dominating presence that Sam had. I knew it was stupid of me to compare everyone to Sam, but that is where my brain went instantly. I realized that Ian was the first person I had fucked with since Sam, but I had felt a connection with Sam that I didn't think anyone was going to be able to live up to.

Ian got into the rhythm of fucking and began to use my hips to slide myself over his hard cock as he watched. I could hear him groaning and mumbling to himself, but I had my head buried in the couch cushions mostly, so it was hard to hear. He lasted longer this time, and when he finally came, he continued to plow into me through his climax.

"Fuck me!" he finally yelled as he collapsed onto my back, sweaty and breathing hard.

"Awesome," I complimented him. "You got one more in you?" I knew I was giving him very little recovery time, but I had been spoiled by Sam, who seemed never to go limp.

"Jesus. I didn't know it would be like this."

"Like what?" I asked, curious.

"I just didn't know you would be the one that was in charge, I guess. I thought you would be the one that was just grateful to have me fuck you and then would be in the throes of passion, I guess."

I laughed. "Boy, you were sure wrong about that."

"Yeah, I was."

"Not that I'm not grateful to have you fuck me, but I'm not one of those people that sit back and wait for things to happen to me. I'm the kind that makes things happen."

"I see that. You're trying to milk me dry."

"Is that possible?" I asked with a laugh. "Okay, I'll tell you what. If you are capable of going again, I will let you choose what we do and you can direct it. How's that?"

"Sounds good." Ian pulled out of me and I turned around to face him without sitting down on the couch.

"I think I want you on top of me like when we first started . . ." He was suddenly very shy with this request.

"Me sitting on your lap facing you?"

"That's it."

"You mean like this?" I asked as I straddled his legs and massaged his cock with my ass.

"Yeah." Ian moaned with his head back on the sofa. His cock was getting hard under me and I was enjoying running my hands all over his chest and arms. He had a sheen of sweat on his skin that I couldn't resist, so I broke down and licked his big biceps, tasting the delicious sweat.

Ian stared into my eyes and then put both his hands on each side of my face and held me still. "Fuck, you are doing things to me that I never dreamed could be done."

Unfortunately, I had seen that look on his face before. I was bewitching him, but I was just doing this for fun, so I needed to be careful. I didn't want to hurt him or lead him on, but I already knew that this was going to be it for Ian, except for tomorrow, of course. To break the spell, I stood up off him and walked to the kitchen, getting us two more beers. Bringing them back to the end table, I sat back down on Ian's legs and saw that he was fully hard again.

"You ready to go?"

"You bet."

Neither of us needed to be lubed, so I just reached back and slid him up into me. I watched his face as he entered me and saw the pure joy crossing it. Knowing that I was probably tighter in this position, I saw that confirmed on Ian's face. I put my knees up beside his thighs on the couch and began to rock back and forth on him.

Ian reached around and put one big hand on each of my ass cheeks, pulling them apart, therefore driving himself into me further than ever. After a few minutes, I wrapped my arms around his thick neck and whispered to him, "Fuck me hard, Ian."

Ian responded by fucking up into me with speed and depth. It left me almost breathless and I found myself panting on his shoulder. Ian mixed it up on me—slowing way down and slow-fucking me after banging me hard.

I guessed that he was going to take longer to reach his climax this time since it was his third, so he was compensating. At this point, I didn't care, because Ian was scratching that itch deep in my ass that I needed scratched.

I purposely started to rub my semi-hard cock on his chest, loving the feeling of my cock hardening and my asshole sliding up and down on Ian's long pole. My climax was building, and based on Ian's heartbeat, I thought he was getting close as well.

"Fucking give it to me," I encouraged him.

He let out a primal scream and pulled my ass down onto his crotch with one swift move. I let go of his neck and leaned back, arching into space. With one hand I grabbed my cock and begun to jack myself off. Ian exploded with his climax, shooting hot cum all over my anal channel. He grunted as he spasmed, shooting more spunk with each wave of sensation.

Finally, I was able to join him, shooting my load onto his chest in big thick strands. I made sure that I didn't hit his face or neck. Since he was a NOMAR, I didn't want him freaking out on me. My ass muscles clamped shut with my climax and I squeezed his cock with force, milking the last few drops from him.

"Nice workout, Ian."

"Hell fucking yes, it was!"

I stood up and asked, "Do you want to shower before you go?"

"I've taken up enough of your time already. I'll shower at home. Thanks so much."

I grabbed a rag out of a laundry basket in the corner of the room and wiped him down. I wiped his cock and crotch as well as my own before he got dressed. Ian left, already thinking about tomorrow. I was thinking of Sam as I showered Ian off of me.

Chapter Eighteen

Sunday morning brought the excitement of the Pirates game and the visit of Ian, Jordy, and Jay. I had just gotten out of bed, slapping on a robe, and was in the kitchen making coffee when there was a knock on the door.

"Who the hell is this?" I muttered as I headed to the door. I was not a morning person, and my least favorite thing to do in the morning was to talk. I opened the door and there stood an older guy who looked more accountant than anything else.

"Hey! I'm Jonas, your neighbor." He pointed to the house to the right of mine. "I noticed you moved in and I wanted to invite you over to lunch today to meet my family."

Suddenly he noticed my mark and his mouth hung open. This told me more than anything else that he was trying to be nice without any further agenda, which was good, because he was not attractive.

"I'm Brand. That's really nice, but I don't want to impose," I said politely.

"No imposition. My boys and I are going to church and then we'll be ready to eat at one o'clock. Does that work for you?"

"You have sons?" If he had kids, then that would make the whole situation safer for me.

"Yes, two."

"Sure, thanks so much, Jonas."

"Okay. See you then." I watched him go back to his house. I got the impression that he was a good guy, and I guessed I would see this afternoon when I spent some time with him.

I finished the coffee and read a little bit while I enjoyed it. As the clock approached one, I showered and dressed for lunch. I figured they wouldn't mind if I wore shorts, since the day was so fucking hot. I put on some dress shorts and a nice button-down shirt and walked over to the house next door.

Jonas answered my knock with a huge smile on his face. "I was afraid you wouldn't come. I mean I wouldn't have blamed you." He showed me into the living room. "I mean, I didn't realize that you were marked when I invited you and I wouldn't blame you for going into a house of NOMARs that you didn't know." His nerves were showing.

"No problem. I felt better about coming when I realized that you didn't know."

"Brand, this is my oldest son Jim." I shook Jim's hand. He was my age, tall and skinny. He looked very average in every way, but had a friendly smile and a firm handshake.

"Nice to meet you, Jim."

"You, too. When dad told me that the new neighbor was marked and that you were coming to lunch, I was in shock. But here you are."

Jonas continued, "And this is my youngest, Bryce." Jim moved out of the way and there standing behind the couch was a bright-eyed, brown-haired Adonis. "He just graduated from high school last month. It still feels weird to introduce an eighteen year-old man as my youngest kid."

"Hi, Bryce," I said, holding out my hand.

"Hey." He shook my hand with force, and I felt the sexual tension between us immediately. His hand was large and meaty and he was wearing a tank top that showed off big biceps that were muscular without any definition, in a way that only could have been said of an eighteen year old body.

Jonas ushered me around the couch and had me take a seat. "What can I get you to drink?"

"Water's good."

Jim and Bryce sat down across from me. I could now see that Bryce was wearing cargo shorts and was barefoot. His feet were big and flat, reminding me of Fred Flintstone's, and the left one turned in slightly just to drive me out of my mind, since I had a fetish for that particular thing. He was a thick-bodied kid without being fat. His brown hair was shaggy without any part or rule to it.

"So, where are you from, Brand?" Jim asked as he sat down.

"Originally from South Carolina, but I've lived in Boston for the last couple of years."

"And what brings you to the 'Burgh?"

"I have some friends who have either moved here or are from here."

"That's cool," Jim commented. I couldn't help but see that Bryce was staring a hole through me like he wanted to throw me down right there on the couch. It made my crotch tingle with excitement, and I felt my dick starting to come alive.

"Do you go to school?" I asked Jim. I couldn't quite make out his age.

"No, I play in a band on the weekends and work landscaping during the week. Bryce is going to go to Duquesne in the fall."

"That's cool," I said to Bryce. "Did you get a lot of presents for graduation?"

"One big one," Jim crowed.

Bryce's huge mouth formed into a brilliant smile. "Most people don't wear watches anymore, but I really like them, so Jim and my dad got me a really expensive watch that I've been wanting."

"Is it the one you have on now?"

"No, I'll show it to you after lunch." His face told me that he had more than a watch to show me after lunch.

"Cool." Jonah was back with the drinks and we moved to

the dining room table.

Dinner was fried chicken and all the fixings. Jonah admitted that he had bought it from the local grocery store instead of cooking it himself, but I didn't care, because it was good. Dessert was cobbler. The boys had a lot of questions about me and I had a lot about the neighborhood, so the time seemed to really fly.

I was almost finished with my last bite of the berry cobbler when Bryce said, "I'll show you my graduation watch now if you want to see it."

"Sure." I ate the last bite and followed him to a room off the hallway leading into the back of the house.

Bryce led me into his bedroom. It was small and it struck me as strange that he had a large collection of high-top sneakers that he had displayed on top of their boxes along one whole wall of his room. He opened the top drawer of his dresser and pulled out a watch box. It looked very expensive.

When he opened the box, I was having trouble concentrating on the watch because I was standing very close to Bryce and could smell his manly scent. I could also see his amazing feet on the carpet directly below. The watch was beautiful and looked like it had cost a couple of thousand dollars.

"It's very nice, Bryce. I mean, I don't know anything about watches, but it's beautiful."

"Thanks." He beamed. "Now, walk out to the dining room and ask to use the bathroom."

I was startled at first and then I realized he had a plan.

"Okay, and then what?"

"Go to the bathroom."

Easy enough, I thought to myself as I turned and headed back to the dining room. I was rarely in a position to be commanded, and had never expected an eighteen-year-old to be able to do so. I asked Jonas if I could use the restroom and then followed his directions to get to it. I walked inside, marveling at how similar it was to the one in my house. I closed the door and then saw Bryce standing against the sink behind the shower.

"Hey," I said, startled.

Bryce didn't say anything, but pointed at the toilet which I sat down on. He unbuttoned his shorts and pulled them and his boxers down, stepping out of them. He pulled his tank top off and I bent forward, running my hands all over his chest and arms. His cock was nice and thick like the rest of him, but a little bigger than average in length.

I wrapped my hand around his semi-stiff cock and pulled on it. Bryce grinned that terrific grin, and I bent further towards him to suck his cock into my hot mouth. He tasted fresh and delicious, like he had just showered. I heard him groan quietly as I started to pull on his penis skin with my mouth, beginning to suck him off.

Bryce hardened instantly, and I pulled his cock out of my mouth so I could get the measure of it. It was a nice fat cock and I massaged it with my hand as I sucked on his balls. He groaned more and grabbed my shoulders with his big hands. Spitting out his balls, I moved onto his cock again and pistoned back and forth on him until he exploded in a quiet eruption in my mouth. His boy-cum was sweet and delicious and I sucked him for all I was worth.

Pulling his cock out of my mouth, I ran my thumb up the vein on the bottom of it and milked several more pearls of cum from his fuck-stick. I flicked them off his cock head with my tongue and looked up at him.

"Very nice," Bryce whispered while intently looking down at me. "I need to fuck you tonight."

God, he was forward. "No, I have plans tonight."

"Cancel them." His face showed no sign of emotion except for lust.

"I can't," I said as I stood up.

"Then afterwards."

"No." I was in charge of my schedule, whether he wanted to admit it or not. He didn't look disappointed like I thought he would, but instead he was smiling. "Maybe we could grab some lunch tomorrow."

"I am at your service," he said as he bowed to me.

Freaky, but kinda cute. I would fuck with him and then cut him off. There was no future with this kid. I got up, washed my hands, drank some of the tap water, and turned and looked at Bryce while I left the restroom.

Walking back to the kitchen, I said to Jim and Jonas, "Sorry guys, I think I might have a little bug." I was trying to cover my long absence. "Thank you so much. It was nice to meet you guys, and it will be my turn to cook for you next."

"Hope you feel better."

"Me, too."

Jonas yelled, "Bryce, Brand's leaving."

Bryce appeared, having completely changed clothes. I guess he figured that explained his absence. "Nice to meet you, Brand." He grinned as he shook my hand.

They walked me to the door and watched me go inside my front door. For the next couple of hours, I couldn't help but process what had just happened. Straightening up the house, I got prepared for the guys to come over. I was planning on ordering some pizza after they got here, but for appetizers I put out some bowls of Cracker Jacks and chips.

I was lost in thought when I heard the knock on the door. Opening it, I saw Ian, Jordy, and Jay in their Pirate gear.

"Hey guys!"

"Hey!" they all said, grinning from ear to ear.

I got them all a beer and we sat down in front of the game. After the first inning, a weird sort of silence settled in amongst us. I knew that they were all amped up about what they *hoped* would happen, but now that they were in the thick of it, they didn't know how to get it started. I ordered the pizza and it was delivered pretty quickly. We wolfed it down, talking excitedly about the game while we ate.

Finally, taking pity on them, I asked, "So, when do you guys wanna start fucking?" There was complete silence and each of them wore a mask of stunned disbelief.

Ian was less apprehensive than the rest, so he said, "Well, boys, what do you think?"

"I think we're good whenever you are, Brand," Jay said.

"We can turn the game on upstairs in the bedroom."

"Awesome," Jordy said.

"Let's grab some beers and then we'll head upstairs," I said, decisively.

They followed me like ducklings in a line up the stairs, each of us clutching two beers. I showed them the bedroom with my king-sized bed and eighty-four-inch plasma HDTV on the wall. Using the remote, I turned to Root Sports, and the game popped on the screen in brilliant greens and browns.

I turned around to see that the three guys were already undressing and soon they were high-fiving each other. Stripping also, I soon found myself on my knees in front of them, moving from one cock to another. They were all hard before we even began, so I didn't have to work any magic and they all seemed to think I was doing miracles.

Ian was the first to make a move, reaching down and pulling me up by the armpits. He pushed me back onto the bed, lifted my legs up onto his broad shoulders and lubed us both. Jay and Jordy both watched in amazement as Ian entered me, split my anal ring, and pushed into me. This was the first time that Ian had fucked me in this position, and I had to admit that I was loving it. His big body was pressing me into the mattress, and I held onto his rippling biceps as he destroyed my ass.

"Fucking tearing me up, Ian."

He laughed, then turned to Jay and Jordy. "One of you fucks wanna stick your cock in his mouth to keep it busy for me?"

We all burst out laughing and they came over and knelt on either side of my head. I turned my head to one side and sucked Jay and then turned it to the other side and greedily sucked Jordy.

It must have been quite a sight to see, because Ian increased his speed and was almost on the verge of recklessness in his thrusting. He couldn't keep up the pace and soon pulled out and shot his load on my cock and balls. It was hot to be splashed with his man-goo as he jerked himself above me. I was glad that I had put a couple of towels on the bed earlier, which I used now to clean myself up.

"That was so fucking . . . amazing," Jay said, astonished.

"It is amazing. Your turn, Jordy," Ian said happily.

After some shuffling around, Jordy held up one of my legs, turned me onto my side, and entered me while standing on the floor beside the bed. Jay put his cock back into my mouth from the other side of the bed, effectively spit-roasting me on my side. Jordy's cock was average in every way, but he had a real graceful fucking style that was nice to experience, especially after Ian's frantic one.

Ian brought his meat up for me to clean the cum off him, so Jay stepped out of the way and I sucked Ian clean. He started to get hard again, just as Jordy begun to grunt and then blew a load of hot cum inside me. Jay was next and he wanted me to sit on his lap, so he propped his back against the headboard with pillows and I let gravity impale me down onto his hooked cock. It felt good inside me as the hook in his cock probed my prostate with each thrust. I held onto the top of his bald head as I raised and lowered myself on his fuck-stick.

Ian stepped up onto the mattress and let me suck him. Jay

held me suspended above his crotch and fucked up into me as hard and as fast as he could. He was panting hard from the exertion when he came, shooting hot strands of his spunk deep into my anal channel. Ian didn't waste any time, reclaiming my ass for his own. He fucked me standing against the wall in a more subdued, controlled manner this time. When he came this time, he, once again pulled out and shot his load onto my bubble butt. Ian seemed to really get off on watching his cock pump that salty cum onto me.

Jay and Jordy each fucked me one more time before we all took time in the shower to get clean. All the guys were very happy and thanked me a million times for letting them come over.

Ian hung back when the other two went downstairs. "Can I come over tomorrow?"

"Ian, I don't want to lead you on, but this is kinda a two-time deal."

He was silent while his brain tried to register what I was saying.

"I mean, I'll keep your number and it's possible we might hook up another time, maybe, but I'm not promising anything."

"You didn't like it?" he asked, his voice so quiet that I almost didn't hear him.

"I had fun, but you're not the man I'm going to see every day." He looked totally dejected. "I'm sorry, but I have to go with my feelings on this."

"Okay." He turned to head down the stairs. "But you will keep my number?"

"Of course."

I walked the guys to the door, said goodbye, and locked it behind them. I was just thinking how awkward that conversation had been with Ian when I noticed movement out of the side window beside the door. I looked onto Jonas' front porch. Bryce was standing in the shadows, watching the guys leaving my house, getting into their cars, and driving away.

It made a shiver run up my spine and I made sure he did not see me through the window as I climbed the stairs to change my bed and go to sleep.

CHAPTER NINETEEN

Right before going to bed, I put my cell phone into the charger and saw that I had a message from Crash asking if we were still on for tomorrow night. I sent him a text back that we were and included my address.

I spent the morning cleaning up from the Pirates party the night before. Afterwards, I took a hot bath in Epsom salts to loosen up my stiff muscles. It had been quite a workout yesterday and I had a feeling that today was going to be just as intense.

At eleven o'clock on the dot, there was a knock on my door. I opened it to see Bryce standing on my stoop wearing a huge smile. "Hey, Bryce."

"Whattsup?"

"You ready for lunch?"

I figured that he had been chomping at the bit since we made the plans. He'd probably told himself to wait until eleven and then he couldn't wait any longer. I personally felt a rumble in my stomach, as well as the familiar itch in my ass and the sexual spark between us.

"Yeah."

He rubbed his stomach as he came in. He was in shorts and a t-shirt with a ridiculous day-glow orange baseball cap on his head that had a wide flat brim. Bryce was wearing one of his pairs of unique hi-tops that were orange with blue trim. I shut the door behind him and told him that I was almost ready. I put on flip-flops and grabbed my wallet and keys off the kitchen counter.

"Jonas and Jim at work?"

"Yeah. I'm home alone." he smirked.

"Me, too," I said as I walked out of the house. "You wanna drive my car, since you know the city better than me?"

"Sure." I threw him the keys and we drove to a Pittsburgh landmark restaurant known as Primanti's. I had seen it on TV when I watched the Steelers play and I was excited to be eating there. They were famous for piling their sandwiches with tons of meat, slaw and French fries, right on the sandwich.

Bryce and I ordered and then settled in to wait.

"So, how did your plans work out last night?" he prompted.

"Good," I answered, wary of him, but curious as to where he was going with this.

"I saw them leave," he said flatly.

"I saw you see them leave," I returned his flat tone.

"I didn't like it," he said.

"Why not?"

He considered it for a minute. "I thought we had a thing."

"We do, but I also have a thing with other guys."

"That's the part I don't like."

"I don't belong to anyone, Bryce. I can tell you that there is no future with us, either, so if you are going to get weird or too attached, then we can't do this." I knew I was being blunt and a little harsh, but I needed to say this now and set the boundaries.

"You haven't seen me fuck yet," he said with confidence.

"No, but I know enough about myself to know that I'm not going to fall for an eighteen-year-old that I have little in common with, no matter how good you fuck."

"We'll see."

I sat back, smiling at him. He was one of the most confident young guys I had ever met, and I was intrigued by him, despite myself. Our food came and it was just as awesome as promised. Bryce wasn't one for conversation. We ate quickly, finished, and I paid the bill.

Bryce drove us back to my house, and I indicated that I wanted to go to his room. He was a little surprised, but consented. He unlocked the door and opened it wide for me. As soon as he closed it behind us and locked it, he was on me. Surprising me with his actions, Bryce pressed his body into mine and pressed me up against the solid wall behind me. He grabbed each of my wrists and held them up above my head. He was all smiles as he held me there.

I wasn't sure how I felt about him. He interested me and we certainly had some kind of sexual tension between us that was worth exploring. And then he kissed me. This was unexpected. Bryce's lips were full and his mouth was large, so I felt at first that I was being swallowed by him. His kiss was forceful and urgent, knocking the breath out of me. He had his tongue in my mouth before I could even process what was happening, and I responded with the only thing left to me. I moved my body against his, feeling his rock-hard cock between his legs with my knee.

Bryce made small groaning noises into my mouth and then broke free from me, releasing me as he did. "Upstairs," he commanded.

I grabbed the stair railing and began to climb.

He smacked my ass with a flat hand and said, "I'm going to fucking tear that ass up in just a minute."

I wondered where he was getting his confidence from when he ushered me into a bedroom with a king-sized bed in it.

"This is my dad's room," he said, as if answering my unasked question.

"I wanna go to your room," I said to him.

"This is a bigger bed." He had given this some thought.

"What's it matter? One of us is going to be on top of the other one anyway."

Bryce smiled broadly and said, "True, but why my room?"

"I have a thing for feet . . . and shoes." I felt the heat bloom on my neck and ears. This was the first moment where I truly felt vulnerable in front of him.

"So, you liked my shoes on display yesterday?"

"Yes."

"And what about my feet?"

"They are so fucking hot," I said honestly.

"They are?" he looked down at his feet, still encased in his orange hi-tops.

"Oh, yeah!" I laughed as I took his hand and pulled him out of the room and back downstairs. I went back to where I remembered his room to be and realized that his smell was also a lure for me to be in his room. It smelled like a combination of sweat, feet, dirty clothes, and cum. It was intoxicating!

I looked at his shoes all lined up again and I dropped to my knees. Lifting up one of his feet onto my thigh, I began to take his sneaker off and then pulled his sock off. I repeated the process with the other foot as he pulled his shirt off and then my own. The smell of his feet was heady in my nostrils, almost making me swoon. I rubbed each foot before undoing his shorts and pulling them down to the hardwood floors.

"Suck me."

I didn't say anything, but opened my mouth and sucked him in. He tasted great and was so fucking hard, I thought I might hurt him by bending his cock out to get it in my mouth. I slobbered all over his knob.

"Stand."

I spit his cock out and stood up. He planted a kiss on my lips and then crushed me with another one as he pushed my shorts to the floor.

"On the bed on your stomach." Bryce reached for a bottle of lube in the nightstand drawer and I heard him jacking his cock with it. He didn't bother lubing me, but I was sure after last night that I was probably okay without it.

Bryce spread my ass cheeks and inspected my rosebud. He ran a finger over it and then pushed it inside without any warning. I grunted with the pain of it and moaned with the pleasure as he moved it.

"Very nice," he said, as he climbed between my legs.

I felt his cock head resting at my hole and then he reached up to my head and pushed my face into his tennis shoe that I had just taken off. He held it flat in his hand, putting my nose and mouth inside the shoe just as he entered me. The smell of his shoe was strong—making my eyes water and my cock hard. His cock was stretching my anal ring with its girth and he kept pushing until he was completely buried inside me.

Bryce dropped the shoe on the bed under my face and grabbed both of my shoulders, pulling me up and back. He proceeded to fuck me hard and fast, occasionally leaning down to turn my head and kiss me. He came fast and was left me panting as he rubbed my back and used my hips to milk the rest of his cum out of his cock.

"How'd you like that?"

"It was hot," I admitted.

"Fucking straight, it was!" He wrapped his arms around my waist and rolled me on top of him as he rolled over onto his back. Bryce spread my legs with his while I leaned my head over his shoulder. He begun to fuck me again and I was impressed that he hadn't even gone limp.

Bryce gave me another hard fucking, from below this time, as I held my cock and balls up against my stomach to keep them out of the way. He grunted loudly with his second climax and let me settle down onto his crotch while he recovered.

"Fucking nice hole," Bryce finally said, as he returned to himself.

"I have to admit that you are an exceptional fuck. Where did you learn how to do it?"

He was silent for a moment and then said, "An older marked guy showed me what to do the first time."

An alarm went off in my head. "Older?"

"Yeah. He didn't really have any experience, either, so we fumbled through it together."

That made me feel better, but I was still getting a weird vibe from him.

"We got pretty good at it the more we practiced. Two years later, a kid in my class got his mark and I seduced him into letting me show him what we could do. From then on out, I pretty much fucked those two every week. After that, another kid in my school got his mark and he sought me out to teach him. I guess the word had gotten around," he said, pride coloring his words.

"I guess," I said, not feeling as impressed with him as he was with himself.

Bryce pushed me up and off of him. He stood up and laid me down on my back, pulling me to the edge of the bed while putting my ankles on his shoulders. "How many times did you get fucked last night?"

He'd shocked me again. "None of your business."

He smiled broadly. "I figured that each one of them probably fucked you twice, so, I have to at least drop seven loads in you to make you mine." Before I could say anything he entered me again, causing me to arch my back and bite down on my lip.

When I had myself under control, I said, "Bryce, I'm not going to be yours. I thought I had made that clear."

"You did, but that was before this," he said, indicating our bodies hooked together.

"Even now. I still believe it."

He leaned between my legs and planted his mouth on mine, pressing down. When he pulled back, he said, "You'll come around."

Bryce began to fuck me hard from on top of me, bending my legs back onto myself as he did push-ups into me. His pace was slower this time and more methodical. When he reached his climax, I felt his cum start to exit with each stroke and run down my ass and onto the bed.

Bryce fucked me once more, doggy-style, before he ran out of steam. I had been impressed by him when not many people impressed me, but he had a big enough head already, so I didn't tell him. He wanted me to stay longer, but I was insistent that I had to go, so I jumped in his shower, got dressed, and went home.

I saw Bryce drive off a half-hour later and wondered if I had just made a huge mistake. I sent Crash a text that maybe I should meet him at a restaurant and we agreed on the Tilted Kilt in Robinson.

Looking forward to having some mature conversation, I soaked in a hot tub again at my house. I seriously needed to evaluate how this was going. I still missed Sam a lot and I realized that I was looking for him in every guy and that I was fucking to keep myself from missing him, but I didn't think it was working. I thought of Sam more than I'd ever thought of anyone, including my imaginary Master whom I had dreamed up when I was thirteen.

I pulled into the parking lot at the Tilted Kilt and saw Crash leaning against his truck. He was all cleaned up with a new graphic t-shirt on with dress shorts and sandals. He wasn't wearing a hat, and I was pleased to see that his brown hair was cut into a faux-hawk that I just wanted to run my hands through, it looked so thick.

"Hey," I yelled to him.

His head turned and I watched his face light up. "How's it going?" he asked as we walked towards the door.

"Good. How was work today?"

"Hot," he snorted.

We ate some good Irish food and drank some Guinness. The conversation between Crash and I never really seemed to wane, even as we laughed at the servers in kilts and the looks we were getting from the other patrons. I paid the bill and we went to the parking lot.

"Wanna go to your place?" I asked. I watched his face fall.

"I . . . just have a little apartment."

"That's cool. I'm having a little problem at my house at the moment, and I really don't care where you live."

"Okay." His face brightened and he smiled again. "Wanna ride with me?"

Patrick had always taught me to be a little wary of getting caught somewhere without wheels, so I said, "I'll follow you." We drove to a low-end apartment complex in Moon and parked in front of it.

"This is it," Crash said as an apology.

"It's not bad," I said, looking around.

"You're nice, but I bet you are used to a lot better than this," he said, his face downcast.

"Crash, I can tell you that I've stayed in some of the most expensive hotels and houses in the US, and they are not always better than this."

He brightened a bit and walked me to his apartment, which he unlocked and led me into. Crash's apartment was pretty sparse, with nothing on the walls and not much furniture.

"I don't spend a lot of time here," he said, still sounding apologetic.

He grabbed us each a beer and walked me back to the bedroom. As soon as he opened the door, I could tell this was his sanctuary. The carpet was thicker, the walls were painted a bright blue, and the plasma screen TV looked big and new. He had no bedroom furniture at all, not even a bed. He did have a mattress which was just on top of the box springs, lying on the floor, but his mattress was made and the comforter and sheets looked new. There was a huge mirror on the sliding closet doors.

"This is nice."

"Yeah, I've been working on this room." I could see the pride on his face as I heard it in his voice.

"You've done a nice job."

"Thanks." He walked over and grabbed a remote and turned on the TV. He muted it and said, "Want me to put some porn on?"

I laughed. "I'm cool with that if you want to." I had rarely watched any porn because I was having so much sex. Patrick wasn't a porn fan, and he found the latest craze, of multiple masked NOMARs fucking a marked guy against his will, disgusting.

Crash's eyes twinkled with delight as he grabbed a couple of DVDs from a box in the closet. "I have traditional and non-traditional," he said with a grin.

I figured traditional was probably two marked guys having sex, or a Servant and a Master. I wasn't sure what non-traditional was, so I decided on that. Crash put it in and switched the input on the screen while I lay down on his bed. He pulled his t-shirt off and lay down beside me. His body was incredible, and I was just about to touch it when the TV screen flickered to life on the security warnings.

This *movie*, if you could call it that, was about a marked guy who was abducted and then woke up in an abandoned house. He was disoriented and scared, finding a tape recorder that told him that he was being tested. As he moved through the house, he would have a series of obstacles to overcome as he made his way to freedom.

It was an intriguing concept, and I smiled easily to Crash to let him know that I was enjoying it. He looked relieved.

The marked guy on the screen had come to the first obstacle, which was a series of cocks sticking through glory holes. He had a set amount of time to get them all to spill their loads. I laughed and turned my attention to Crash. I couldn't wait to run my hands over his chiseled chest, so that was what I did. He looked at me with a mix of longing and lust on his face.

I squeezed his nipples and teased them with my fingertips before I pulled my shirt off and leaned over his chest, sucking his nipples into my mouth. Biting and sucking on them, I heard Crash gasp and then hold his breath. I moved over and crawled on top of him, using my arms and legs to hold myself above him. I licked his abs and then his hairy treasure trail as I unbuttoned his shorts and pulled them and his jock strap down. He kicked them off, and I continued my relentless assault of him with my tongue.

His cock popped up into my face, begging for attention. It was a really nice dick, reminding me of Sam's, but not as thick. He had a very small cock head on that big shaft, giving his member the look of a tapered candle. I sucked the velvety soft cock head into my mouth and used my tongue to tease it. Exploring the lip of his cock head and the pee hole, I left no area untouched.

Crash moaned as he laid his hands on my shoulders, urging me to blow him. I gave in and attempted to swallow him, coming up just short. He had a nice piece of sausage and I pulled him out of my mouth and ran my lips and tongue up and down his shaft while using my thumb to put pressure on the big vein on the bottom of his cock.

"Holy Christ!" Crash yelled as his cock throbbed in my mouth, signaling that he was coming. I pulled everything but his tiny cock head out of my mouth, just as he erupted in me.

He shot thick, ropy strands of hot cum that I swallowed down to keep from choking. He totally let me take control during that blowjob, not trying to thrust into me from below like most NOMARs would have done.

I cleaned him up and said, "Delicious, man."

"Wow," was all he could say as he put his hands over his head on the pillow. We both had a light sheen of sweat on our bodies and I saw on the screen that the marked hero had made it to the next challenge. In this one he had to get in a sling and impale himself on a two-foot dildo anchored to the wall. In order to get out of this room, he would have to pull himself closer and closer to the door, thereby impaling himself further and further onto the dildo.

Better him than me.

I stood up and did a slow strip of the rest of my clothes. Crash's gaze never left my body and he whistled as I turned, giving him a good view of my ass. He licked his lips and asked, "How do you want to fuck?"

"I'll ride you first, if you don't mind."

"How could I mind anything? This is the greatest day of my life." His smile was infectious, and I laughed despite myself.

"Your cock is a thing of beauty. I can't wait to ride it."

"You and me both," he said, laughing. "There's lube in the bathroom."

I stepped into the adjacent room and retrieved a bottle of lube from the shelf above the toilet and rejoined Crash. The marked hero had just completed his second task, virtually impaling himself on a broom stick to do it. I squirted the lube on my hand and jacked Crash's substantial cock. Even though I had already been fucked several times earlier in the day, I knew I was going to need to be slick in order to handle Crash's giant monster.

"You wanna lube me, Crash?" He seemed like an adventurous guy to me, judging from his porn.

"Sure, but I'm not sure how." He seemed excited about it.

I bent over beside him on the bed and gave him instructions. He followed them to a tee and was soon finger-fucking me with gusto. I was panting as he finger-banged me until I couldn't take it anymore and moved away from him.

Crash wiped his hand on some *Kleenex* and I saw that the porn star had moved to the next room. Now he had to drink a gallon of cum in order to retrieve a key inside the jar. I didn't think I could watch, which I wasn't planning on anyway.

Climbing up onto the bed on my knees, I straddled Crash, pushed his cock head into my ass, and slid down his big pole. I watched his face as gravity pulled me down, and I saw the look of sheer pleasure. My ass hole stretched around his shaft as it stroked him and then I was completely impaled on his meat stick. Sitting on his crotch, his pubic hair tickling my buttocks, I ground my hips and ass around on him.

Crash moaned and groaned as he held my hips with his sweaty hands and pushed his head back into the pillow. I rose and lowered myself on him, bracing my upper body with my arms, which were anchored on his giant pecs. Soon we were both moaning and sweating as we hit our stride, Crash punching deeper and deeper into me, milking his shaft in the tight grip of my ass hole.

"Oh, fuck!" Crash gritted through clenched teeth as he pulled my hips down and simultaneously thrust his cock upward and exploded inside me. His body rocked with his climax, and I rode each spasm like I was straddling a surf board at North Myrtle Beach.

I thought to myself, while I continued to wiggle on him, that his cock almost felt like Sam's in me, but Crash was a completely different guy than Sam in the approach. Crash was perfectly content to let me direct him and take charge, as well as do all of the work. Sam wouldn't let me do any of those things, even when I wanted to. There was also a sense of suspense with Sam that I had never found with anyone else. He constantly surprised me in a time when that seemed to have gone away. And then there was the connection. No one had ever felt as connected to me, so fast or so completely, as Sam did. I didn't even know how to describe it, but now that I had experienced it, I needed to find it again.

"That was fucking mind-blowing," Crash said, as he ran his flattened palm up my stomach and chest.

"It was pretty good, wasn't it?" I teased him. "Can you go again?"

"I'm sure I can."

"Why don't you roll us over," I directed and then explained what we were going to do. Crash followed my directions and was soon on top of me while I was on my back and I wrapped my legs around his waist.

His cock felt bigger and longer from this angle, so I laid my head back to enjoy his long-dicking. I squeezed him with my ass muscles as he tried to pull out each time, sending additional sensations through each of us.

"Fuck me hard, Crash," I commanded him, unwrapping my legs from his back so that he would have total control.

"You don't have to ask me twice," Crash said with enthusiasm. He finally got settled in between my legs and begun to tear me up. My back arched and my ass pushed back on him as I relished this fucking that Crash was giving me.

Fucking Crash seemed to be clearing out the fogginess in my head, as well as anything in my ass, so my mind began to wrap around a plan of action that I needed to do for myself. It was perfectly clear to me, and for the first time in a long time I felt hope and happiness within myself.

CHAPTER TWENTY

Crash was full of thankfulness after we fucked, and me to him, as well. We left as friends and I told him that I would call or text him soon. When I got home, I saw that Jonas' house still had lights on in each room, so I figured that Bryce was watching me from one of the windows.

Sure enough, as soon as I got into the house, there was a knock on the door. I looked out of the peephole and saw Bryce.

Unlocking and pulling the door open, I said, "Bryce."

He nodded his head at me and said, "Did you enjoy yourself tonight?"

"It's late, Bryce. What do you want?" I asked, ignoring his question.

"Just checking on you, unless you want me to come in . . ." He let the rest of the sentence trail off.

"No, I'm good. Thanks for the concern, though. My friend, Patrick, is coming tomorrow to stay with me for a couple of days, so I might see you after that." I closed the door and locked it.

Well, he certainly didn't like hearing that . . .

I showered and went to bed dreaming of my new plan for my life.

I woke with it still in my head, and I was energized for the day. Patrick would be here in a couple of hours and we had a lot to talk about. It would be good to see him again, and I always valued his advice. I was a little nervous about discussing matters of the heart with him, because I didn't want him to feel badly about himself. But in the end, I was pretty sure he would understand.

Making sure the house was clean and tidy first, I showered, dressed in my nicest casual clothes, and picked Patrick up at the airport. We hugged, and he seemed really happy to see me.

"Where are you taking me for lunch?" Patrick asked with a smirk.

"Swickley. It's where the rich and famous go in Pittsburgh."

"Perfect!" Patrick rolled his eyes.

We went to the Swickley Café and enjoyed a wonderful lunch. I told Patrick all about my trip to the beach and what I had been doing since I moved to the 'Burgh. I asked him a lot of questions about what he had been doing and how our friends and his relatives were. We got caught up quickly and finished lunch.

"This is really different."

"What is?" I asked, not understanding him.

"You paying," Patrick said, starting to laugh out loud.

"Thanks to you," I said, giving him all the credit.

"Well, show me your rental."

"All right." We piled in the car and drove to my house. I gave him the tour and then told him about Bryce next door.

Patrick was not happy about that. "It could be dangerous for you," he warned.

"I know. That's why I have to decide where I want to be in my life pretty quickly. I definitely have to leave this house." It was the first time that I had admitted it to myself, and now that I heard it out loud, I knew it was the right move.

Patrick and I sat down at my kitchen table and I outlined my plan to him. He considered all the angles and asked a million questions. I was glad that I had him to use as a sounding board.

Finally, Patrick sat back and said, "Are you sure this is what you want to do?"

"Yes."

"It will tie up a lot of your capital."

"I know, but it will be worth it."

"Are you sure it is a good investment?"

"Yes."

He looked at me as if seeing straight into my heart and soul. "You'll need Eric, and you'll need my lawyer, John."

I got very excited. "So you think it is feasible?"

"Sure, but you need to be sure this is what you want. Once you commit to this, there is no easy way back."

"I wasn't sure until yesterday, and then I had a revelation. Now I'm positive."

Patrick shook his head. "You are just lucky that I am so good with money."

"I know it! I'm a lucky son-of-a-bitch to have been called by you to Service."

"Well, I think we were both lucky on that front."

Patrick and I went out for a nice Italian dinner in Bloomfield and made plans over the pasta. The next day I gave him a tour of the city, including the Strip District, and went for a ride on one of the inclines. I texted Crash, wanting to see if he might be able to come over for dinner tomorrow and meet Patrick. He said he could, so I bought the food I would need for dinner while we were in the strip.

I had not heard from Sam or Michael for a few days, so I started to wonder if they were slowly slipping away. It worried me, but I was fortunate to have Patrick here to distract me. Patrick was easy to talk to and very low maintenance. If I wanted to just veg out in front of the TV, then Patrick was certainly up for that.

Patrick and I hung out until Crash arrived the next night

for dinner. I introduced them and they seemed to like each other immediately. I knew that Crash was just the opposite of Patrick and that he would intrigue him. If I had still been his Servant, Patrick would probably have commanded me to have sex with Crash while he watched. I was sure that was exactly what I was planning anyway.

Dinner was good, and Crash ate like he had been on a deserted island for months. They both complimented me on the food, and I served homemade pound cake for dessert.

"Well, Crash, what do you think about going upstairs and having a little fun?" I asked, hungry for a different kind of dessert.

"With Patrick?" he asked, stunned. I could see the warring going on in his head between wanting to fuck, but not with someone else.

"I like to watch, Crash. If that is acceptable to you," Patrick stated very plainly.

"You wanna watch Brand and I fuck?"

"Yes."

Crash looked at me and said, "Have you done this before?"

"Yes. He's telling the truth. He only wants to watch."

Crash flashed that huge toothy grin. "Okay, then." We all got up from the table and made our way upstairs. Crash loved my old house and told me twice how cool it was. I had already turned the air on in the bedroom, so it was nice and cool by the time we entered. I had also put a nice armchair in the corner for Patrick.

I started by sitting on the bed and undressing Crash, who stood in front of me. His cock was already hard when I pulled his jock off and it bounced up to greet my hungry lips. Patrick kept quiet, but I could hear him shift occasionally to get a better angle from which to see.

Crash groaned at my expert swordplay, eventually grabbing my head in both of his hands and guiding my mouth back and forth on his throbbing member. Just like the last time we had fucked, Crash didn't last long the first time and was soon filling my mouth with his creamy spunk. I swallowed his cream down, loving the taste of it and whining for more when he ran dry.

"God damn!" Crash yelled as he recovered from the sensitive slurping that I was administering to his cock-sickle.

"Was it good for you, Crash?" Patrick asked.

"Fucking fantastic," Crash said, enthusiastically.

"How about for you, Brand?" Patrick asked.

"Very nice." I grinned at Patrick while giving Crash a wink.

Crash looked at me apprehensively. "You want me to fuck you now?"

"Yes, please," I answered.

I laughed to myself. Crash was acting like he was auditioning for a part in one of his porno movies. He was acting like Patrick was the director and that he was supposed to be following a script. I sucked Crash's manhood back into my mouth, pulling on him until he was hard again.

Lying back on the bed, I raised my legs and pointed at the bottle of lube on my nightstand. Crash grabbed it and squirted some on his fingers and then worked them inside of me. He was grinning, and I couldn't help but think it was because he was proud of himself for this new skill he had acquired in our last fuck session. I groaned as he worked those big rough construction fingers inside me and moved them around.

Crash had lubed me enough and then moved onto lubing himself, greasing his cock thoroughly before sidling up to me and putting my ankles on his shoulders. Placing his cock head on my hole, he pushed his hips forward and plunged into my depths. When he reached the end of his shaft, he held us there with his eyes closed, his head back, and his tongue out.

"Fuck me deep and hard, Crash."

Those were the words he must have been waiting to hear, because he took off like a jackrabbit. He held my legs by the ankles and fucked me by rocking back and forth. Then he put my legs on his shoulders and fucked down into me. Then he put my legs on the sides of his hips and fucked me in an undulating manner similar to the way a jellyfish moves. Crash certainly was creative in his approach to fucking this time.

He came hard, sweating and panting between deep thrusts into my sore ass designed to deliver more of his hot spunk into me. He collapsed on the bed beside me still trying to get his breathing under control as I ran a hand languidly over his hard chest.

"That was fucking hot, Crash," I said to him, and meant it.

"Thanks. I never get tired of your sweet ass."

"How was it for you, Patrick?" I asked, trying to include him.

"Very interesting." I wasn't sure what Patrick meant by that, but I was sure that I would find out sooner than later.

Crash was up for one more go, so I rode him this time, facing away from him so that he could sit and watch his big cock slide in and out of me. He seemed to really enjoy that, if his mutterings were any indication. When he came again, it was short and sweet and he was spent.

I showed him where the shower was and we both got cleaned up before saying goodbye to him. I wondered if Bryce was watching at his window. I went back upstairs to the bedroom where Patrick was waiting. This was the part I was a little apprehensive about. How would Patrick and I react in a sexual way since our agreement was over, or would we not? I was dying to find out how it was all going to play out.

Patrick was lying on the bed when I came back into the bedroom. "Well, that was something, wasn't it?"

"I'd like to hear your thoughts . . ."

"Well, Crash is certainly very capable. Good looking, built like a brick shithouse, huge cock . . ."

"Yes, but . . ."

"But he needs to be directed. I know you, and that is your strength, but not your passion." As usual, Patrick hit the nail right on the head and was able to summarize the situation in the plainest way possible.

"I know. I kinda felt like I was in a porn there for a while. He has all the qualities I look for, but not the drive."

"Too bad," Patrick lamented.

"What are we going to do?" I posed to him.

"What do you want to do?"

"Well, are you all worked up from watching Crash fuck me or not?"

"I am."

"Well, so am I, so, let's sixty-nine and take care of each other."

"Sounds like a plan." Patrick was genuinely surprised and overjoyed by my offer. We lay on the bed opposite each other after Patrick had stripped and I blew him while he gave me a hand job. We both came with gusto and lay back taking deep breaths while we recovered ourselves.

Sam got home early from work and marinated steaks for dinner. He placed baking potatoes in the oven, wrapped in foil, as soon as he walked in the house, and now they were almost done. The grill out back was hot, so he carried the steaks outside to grill them, along with a beer to drink.

He heard his father's truck pull up in front of the house and figured he would smell the grill and come around back, but instead he went through the front door into the house. He could hear raised voices in the house, but not what was being said, so he hurried inside.

Cam was standing in the middle of the dining area in the kitchen, and Michael was setting the table. Cam's face was flushed and he looked fidgety. As soon as he saw Sam walk in the back door, he said, "There you are. I've got some news. I had the most amazing day!" His voice was higher and his rate of speech was faster than Sam could ever remember it.

"Dad, what is it?"

"I can't wait to tell you, but I don't want whatever you're grilling to burn, so hurry up and get it off of there and I will tell you."

Sam looked at his father as if he was a stranger, then turned and headed back to the grill. "Good thing we like them rare," he said as he flipped the steaks. He had never seen his dad in this kind of excited state before and he couldn't imagine what was causing it. He pulled the steaks off, turned the grill off, and headed inside.

Michael was just pouring tea in the glasses, and Cam was sitting in his chair at the head of the table, looking over some papers. Michael gave Sam a weird look directed at their dad, but he didn't say anything. Sam put a steak on each of their plates before sitting down. Both he and Michael looked at Cam with piqued curiosity.

"Okay, boys, I need to tell you something that I have been dreading telling you for a long time."

Now Sam was concerned. Was his dad sick?

Cam took a deep breath and said, "Our business has been failing for the last couple of years." He took a dramatic pause and let that sink in before continuing. "I didn't want to admit it at first, and then I tried like hell to save it, asking every bank for loans and refinancing the house, but nothing was working."

"Dad, I didn't—" Sam tried to talk, but Cam put up a hand to stop him.

"This company is my legacy to you two." Cam got tearful

and swiped his eyes with the side of his palm. "When Michael got his mark, I even wondered if he might be able to bail me out, but that was just too far in the future. I tried everything and our week at the beach this summer was all the money I had left."

Sam said quickly, "I figured something was wrong, because you didn't seem to need me as much this year as last."

Cam nodded. "I knew you were onto me and it was only a matter of time before you figured it out or the roof fell in on my head and I had to declare bankruptcy."

"So, what happened?" Michael asked plainly.

"What do you mean?" Sam asked Michael, obviously missing something.

"Well, I don't feel devastation from dad like I would think I should in this situation, so I just assume something has happened." Michael always did have a way of getting right to the point.

Cam laughed. "I can always count on you, Michael, to see the silver lining. So I got a call from the lawyer that the company uses today, and when I called him back, he said that he had been contacted by another lawyer with an offer for me."

Sam and Michael sat in stunned silence, staring at their father.

"I had asked Bernie down at the bank to put some feelers out to see if there was anyone interested in buying the business before I went under. And apparently, there is."

"You would sell, dad?" Sam asked in complete disbelief.

"I would if it meant losing it. I have to leave you boys something for the future." Then he paused dramatically, before saying, "But the good news is . . . I don't have to sell."

"Really?"

"Nope." Cam smiled big. "Walter, the lawyer, came over and met with me for most of the afternoon."

"Well, tell us," Sam said.

"The company wants to invest in us rather than take us over."

"That's cool," Michael said.

"Yeah, it was surprising for me to hear it. But they did have some conditions . . ."

"Uh-oh."

"I thought the same thing, at first."

"So, what are the conditions?" Sam asked, tentatively.

"Well, they think that Lake View has dried up as a viable site for construction, and they are probably right. I have known it for a while that this was true, but I didn't want to admit it."

"So, they want us to move?" Sam asked.

"No way, dad! My friends are all here," Michael said with passion.

"I know, Michael. Our roots are here. They would like the company centered in an area that has more construction potential."

"Like where?" Sam asked.

"Myrtle," Cam said, as if stating the obvious.

"Well, there is a lot of building there," Sam admitted.

"No!" Michael yelled. "I'm not moving."

Cam continued in a level voice. "The company wants to focus on buying high-end properties, renovating them, and selling."

"They want to flip houses?" Sam asked, shock in his voice.

"There's a lot of work for us in that plan. They already have the first property and a buyer for it."

"Well, that's something," Sam said, while shaking his big head.

"It's big time. They are talking million-dollar homes. That's a lot of profit for us."

"How much do they want to be involved?" Sam asked

tentatively, almost afraid of the answer.

"That's the coolest part. They want us to be in charge. SAB has someone that they want to do the interior design, since we are not used to these types of luxury homes, but besides that, it is going to be us."

"SAB?" Sam asked.

"That's the company."

"Fifty-fifty split?"

"Yes."

Sam turned to Michael and said, "It's a really good deal, Michael. I don't think dad can afford to pass it up."

"It's not fair!"

"So, I met with Bernie afterwards and I've made some decisions." Cam let out a big sigh. "I agree with Michael that I think it's not fair to ask him to uproot himself while he's still in school."

"So, you're not going to take the offer?" Sam was absolutely beside himself.

"I'm going to take it, but I'm going to stay here with Michael until he finishes high school or goes to The Service Academy."

"What?"

"Sam, I want you to take over the business. You're ready, and you're totally competent."

"The business is yours, dad."

"And now it is going to be ours. I'm going to scale down the business here, but continue it. I want you to run the Myrtle Beach office."

"Dad, I don't know what to say . . ."

"We're going to be a franchise," Cam said excitedly. "Sam, I want you to take your young guys from the company with you and any of the office staff that want to go, and I'll keep the older guys with me until they retire."

"But, I'll be away from you guys . . ."

"You're only an hour away, and I will be down to check your progress at least once a week. Michael can even spend the summers with you."

Sam thought to himself that maybe even Brand could spend the summer with him. It gave him the impetus to want to try this new adventure. "I'm kinda excited about it," he admitted.

"Why wouldn't you be? Being the boss and having a new direction. It's exciting. So, you'll do it?"

"I'll do it!" Sam said, starting to laugh.

CHAPTER TWENTY-ONE

I started getting the messages and calls from Sam and Michael the next morning. Michael was texting me about all the happenings that his dad had told them about the night before. Sam called me, and we talked for more than an hour about the pros and cons of the deal. I liked that Sam valued my opinion and listened to my observations. I could tell that he was excited about this offer and that he was looking forward to it, but there was something else in his voice.

"What is it, Sam?"

"What do you mean?"

"I can tell there is something else that we're not talking about . . ."

"Well, I just thought that maybe . . ."

"Maybe what?"

"Maybe you and I could spend more time together this way."

"For sure. I would like that. Where's your first job?"

"It's in North Myrtle. Actually, really close to the house you rented."

"That's cool. When are you moving?"

"September. I have a meeting with the interior designer on September the second at the first property."

"Maybe I can fly down in October after you get settled in?"

I heard him exhale on the other side of the phone. "Good. I'll be happy to see you."

"Me, too." We hung up, and I had to admit to myself that I was very happy for Sam. Everything seemed to be going his way and no one deserved it more than he did. It also sounded like his dad and Michael were happy with their decisions as well. I was glad for them and really happy for myself that I might be able to see more of Sam.

I had plans of my own, but I wasn't quite ready to share them with anyone yet, so I had kept quiet about them to Sam and Michael. Feeling a little guilty about that, I sucked it up and dealt with it.

The end of the summer came quickly in Pittsburgh and I got frequent reports from Sam and Michael about the progress of the company move and felt a small part of it. September came, and Sam called me from the hotel he had just checked into in Cherry Grove. He said the beach reminded him of me and our short time together. We talked about my trip down in October and I could tell he was ready to get started working the next day. He reminded me that he had a meeting with the designer in the morning at the work site, which was the house they were going to remodel.

I wished him luck and felt a pang of longing for him after I hung up the phone. I kinda hated that he was in our place without me, if I was going to be honest with myself. Telling myself to just be happy for him and to look forward to October, I went back to work on my plans.

I watched Sam walk into the house only a few doors down from the one we had stayed in last summer. He had driven by the rental house on the way there, and I wondered if he thought about the memories it invoked in me. Now, it was time to get to work.

Earlier this morning, I had watched Sam check out the new offices of his family's construction business. They were modern, spacious, and professional. Sam seemed impressed.

Driving up to the house, I saw that it was on a prime piece

of beachfront real estate and was huge. This house was going to sell for a lot of money.

Having picked up the key to the property at the office, Sam stepped across the threshold into his new job. I was silently hiding in the front closet, peeping through the door slats. He took the opportunity to look around. Seeing a set of blueprints on the kitchen counter, he picked them up and seemed to study them as he walked from room to room, making mental notes to himself. He had just gotten to the master bedroom when he stopped and looked at the blueprints again. I silently left my hiding spot and followed him.

"Why would he need such a big fucking bedroom?" Sam asked himself out loud.

"Because the man he lives with is such a big fucking guy," I said from the doorway.

Sam looked up at me, startled. He didn't say anything, but his eyes were flashing with heat and I could feel the electricity between us like static cling from the dryer. He looked like he couldn't believe what he was seeing. I couldn't believe how hot he was. His skin had retained much of his summer color, and he was still my golden god. He had let his facial hair grow out, and he was now sporting a nice full beard that made him look even sexier than I had remembered. I was so happy to see him that I thought I might burst out laughing or crying.

"Miss me?" I asked.

He rushed towards me, enveloping me in a bear hug. I hugged him back, loving his heat, his smell, and his touch. I felt light-headed and dizzy being this close to him, and there were so many things I wanted to say—and do—to him. Sam pulled back, keeping his hands on my sides. I could see the lust on his face and something else I couldn't place, yet. I immediately reached down and undid the waist button on my jeans and put my hands on his shorts, yanking them down.

Then he was pulling me towards the bed. He pushed me

down on my stomach and yanked my jeans down onto my thighs.

"Well, hello to—" He clamped his big hand over my mouth, effectively silencing me.

The top of my jeans kept my legs firmly tied together, but I lifted my ass up and back towards him. I had never made a better decision than I did this morning to lube my ass before coming to see Sam. He didn't have any lube or spit on his massive cock, but he plunged it into me, anyway. I smashed my eyes shut and saw red and yellow flames of pain as they coursed through my body. Sam slid that magnificent piece of man-meat into me all the way, not stopping until he was buried balls-deep inside me.

"Oh, fuck." I groaned behind his big hand that was still covering my mouth. I knew he couldn't hear or understand my words, but then he didn't really need to. Sam's cock had filled me up completely, just like it had never been anywhere else. It throbbed away in my ass like a ticking time bomb, waiting to go off. I ran my tongue over his big thick fingers and rough palm as it gagged me. I remembered the first time he had fucked me and how I had gotten into trouble for doing this, but I couldn't resist it now.

Sam's skin tasted salty and delicious, and it turned me on like nothing else in the world. Then he started to fuck me. And it was one for the record books. It was like Sam was pissed that he hadn't been able to fuck my little ass for the past two months and now he was going to show it who was the Master. He set a furious pace and I was soon sliding back and forth on the bed, riding his thrusts while grinding my own cock into the mattress.

I bit down on the bottom side of one of his fingers as I withstood the jackhammering of my ass. Sam surprised me by inserting those couple fingers into my mouth, where I continued to bite on the base of them, sucking the rest. He was in his prime, and he was fucking tearing me up with that big cock. I could feel my ass hole start to burn as it was constantly being pushed in and then pulled out by his thrusts, all while sliding up and down at a fast pace on his shaft and being stretched wider than ever by his tremendous girth.

It was a fucking that I would never soon forget, just like the first one we had. The only shard of doubt and insecurity that I might have had about this plan was instantly shattered. Sam was the man for me for the rest of my life, and having his big cock buried inside me was how I wanted it to be forever. I was so happy that I didn't know what to do with myself.

Sucking on his fingers like my life depended on it, I handled Sam's bucking on top of me until I heard him grunt, felt his cock expand slightly inside me, and then felt him bury it to the root in me. He leaned over me, putting his head beside mine. His chin hairs scratched my shoulder as his hot mouth found my earlobe. I knew he was gonna come, so I squeezed his cock with my ass muscles like it was in a vice grip just as he did.

Sam roared with his climax, almost hurting my ears with his bellow. I yelled, too, behind my gag and felt him fill whatever crevices of my ass were free with his hot seed. He pulled his fingers out of my mouth, his hand away from my mouth, and gave me several little mini-thrusts as he grunted with the sensitivity of his post-climatic orgasm before pulling all the way out of me. His beard grazed my cheeks as he moved in and out of me, sending electric currents of stimulation running along my neural pathways.

Minutes later, he pulled back and I, very awkwardly, flipped over, slid to the ground and sucked his messy dick into my mouth, cleaning him up and swallowing his delicious cum down into my gullet. I was having a hard time keeping my tongue and mouth off of his work-of-art cock.

Sam reached down, lifted me up, and whispered, "It's

really you."

"It's me."

"What are you doing here?"

"I'm supposed to meet some lug head contractor here and go over the plans that I have for the inside of this house," I teased him. I knew what he meant, but I was having a good time playing with him.

"You're the designer?"

"Yes."

Suddenly, realization crossed his face. "And you're the company?"

"No." Now, he looked just plain confused. "*We're* the company, you and me . . . SAB."

"What?"

"I want to be with you, Sam, and I want us to be in this together."

"That's what I want also."

I smiled, relieved. "Well, then, that's what we got."

"So, who's house is this?"

"Ours, well, as soon as we get it renovated."

"And until then?"

"I hope you're going to move in with me."

"Where?"

"Our beach house from this summer."

He grinned that big toothy smile and said, "Will we get to do this every day?"

"We will do whatever you want to do, whenever you want to do it, my Master," I answered with a lurid tone to my voice and a bowed head.

At my use of his title, Sam put his head back and sighed heavily. "That was so fucking good. Reminded me of our first time . . ."

"I was thinking the same thing," I said, blushing.

"You were so fucking tight, too. You been saving yourself

for me?"

"Kinda, but you had my jeans restricting my legs from opening, so it was probably just that."

"I'm so happy with you, I don't know what to do."

"How about one more fuck, and then we should get to work. We've got a lot of stuff to do."

"We've got a lot of time to make up for." Sam smirked. "And a lot of fucks . . ."

"One at a time, big boy!"

I laughed as I shucked off my jeans and shirt, watching Sam do the same thing. I drank him in with my gaze, loving his tan and new beard. The time we had spent apart had not diminished our excitement for each other in any way. Lifting my legs, I pulled on his already hardened cock and directed it to my puckered hole.

Sam grabbed both of my ankles in one big hand and pushed them up and back while he pushed his hips forward and entered me. He kept pushing until he could get no more

I could sense that this partnership was going to be the best thing that has ever happened to me. Every part of me was consumed with Sam, and I could tell that every fiber of his being was full of me.

And that's what a partnership is all about.

YOU MAY ALSO ENJOY THE FOLLOWING FROM EXTASY BOOKS INC:

The Dark Master
Crawford Rhine

Excerpt

From the journal of Grayson Edwards—June 15, 2015, at Bucharest, Romania.

Romania is turning out to be quite the treat. I slept really soundly last night after getting hammered by Nick, the guy in charge of security. It felt good to be back on my game again.

The four of us were joined by Florian for dinner. He is Romanian and was hired to act as our interpreter for the trip, even though most of the locals speak excellent English. We ate at a local Romanian restaurant called Haul-Manuc. It was in the courtyard of a very old and very large building that formed the four sides of a courtyard with wooden balconies that ran on several levels completely around.

The food was good—roasted pork, which they called pastrami, and polenta. The wine was even better. Florian talked about our trip, but because James was the detail guy, I only half-listened. Instead, I took in the people of Bucharest, from the violin players entertaining us, the wait staff, the chefs, down to the patrons.

I was surprised that the Romanian NOMARs were so handsome. I had always been a guy attracted to Americans — mostly because I like them rugged and full of confidence. But these Romanians were holding their own. Many of the men had great biceps and well-defined chests that they showed off under tight t-shirts. They fell behind in the leg department, most of them choosing not to work on them in the gym, but overall, they were attractive and mysterious. I like that a lot.

Nick wanted another go after dinner, so I let him fuck me doggy-style while I watched the big hunk lose his shit deep inside me from the giant bedroom mirror. He really is a nice man and a good fuck, but I still went back to my own room to sleep.

I planned on joining the others in the morning like James had instructed.

Worried that I was going to be late, I was relieved to see that I was the second to arrive when I stepped into the hotel hallway. Roger was leaning up against his door with his face already buried in his tablet.

"Morning," I said as I closed my door and looked for a place to prop.

"Morning," he answered without looking up. A few seconds later, he asked, "Where's Nick? You wear him out last night?"

"Excuse me?" I asked in shock.

Roger finally looked up at me. "You played with the bull, and I suppose that you got the horn . . . probably several times, didn't you?"

"It's none of your damn business," I snapped as Nick's door opened and he emerged all in black again. I gave him a withering look and asked, "How do you even know, Roger?"

Roger looked back to his tablet with no concern at all. "I tapped into the hotel security feeds last night. Saw you go into Nick's room and leave an hour later. I just figured it was a good-night fuck. Was I wrong?"

Nick was watching me with an expression between

surprise and humor on his face. "No, you're not wrong. He fucked the shit out of me, and I slept like a baby. You got a problem with that?"

"Nope," Roger said as he held up his hand and high-fived Nick.

"Where's James?" I snapped.

Roger answered me, "He's skipping breakfast . . . not feeling well." When we looked at him questioningly, he said, "He sent me an email."

"Let's go," Nick said, now in charge.

Breakfast was good — croissants with jam, eggs, fruit, cheeses, potatoes, and really strong coffee. I chose to have a latte and sweetened it at the table as Roger and Nick ate heartily. I was never a breakfast guy, so the coffee was my main target. Nick and my extracurricular activities had made me hungry, so I ate a croissant with cheese and some fruit. I would eat something bigger at lunch.

Roger got another email from James while we were eating. "He thinks he might have food poisoning," Roger informed us nonchalantly.

"From last night?" I asked.

"I guess," Roger said.

"I ate the same thing he did," I said worriedly.

"You would have been sick already if you were going to be," Nick informed me.

"What do we do now?" I asked the table.

Roger looked at his tablet, shoveled some muesli into his mouth and said, "He wants us to take the train to Sinaia without him, and he will catch up to us in the afternoon."

"Should we take him to a hospital or something before we leave?" I asked, thinking of how it would feel for me to be left behind sick in a foreign country.

"He's already had the hotel call for a doctor, according to his email."

I was annoyed with this man already, and when I spoke next, it was obvious. "Do you think you can give us all the news at one time, Roger?"

He looked up at me and said, "You chose to give your ass only to some of us, so I can do the same thing with my information if I want to."

"Fuck you," I hissed as I got up from the table and left. My bags were already packed, so I returned to my room and retrieved them. I stopped long enough to write James a get-better-soon note on hotel stationery and slid it under his door.

I waited for Nick and Roger in the lobby with my bags. A taxi took us to the train station where we met Florian. Thank God, he was there, because the woman at the ticket counter did not speak English, and she did not care to even try to understand. We only knew this because a poor Indian man was right in front of us in line, and he was having a terrible time trying to get her to understand what he was saying to her in English.

Florian stepped in and translated for the Indian man and also for us. He handed us tickets for the train and indicated which way to go in the grand building that served as the station. I stopped and bought a bottle of pop for the trip and got a bottle of water for Nick. Roger could fuck himself. I was still mad at him.

Once on the right train, we waited for a few minutes before it departed and then settled in to see the countryside. The train station had been very European to me, and I was excited to see the rest of the countryside. I took the opportunity to start a conversation with the train porter, who sat with us, and he pointed to different points of interests out the windows. His English was decent, and I enjoyed meeting him.

The train soon stopped at the foothills of the Carpathian Mountains at a beautiful little town called Sinaia.

"You have to see Pelles Castle while you are here," Florian told us.

"Maybe after our meetings," I told him. With James out of the picture, I was in charge of the diplomacy and meetings. I should have looked over the paperwork on the train, but I was too interested in seeing the sites. I mainly just had to stall until the afternoon when James would join us.

Nick was taking up the slack from James' absence by taking over the logistics. He got us off the train and into a cab with no problems. I showed the driver the address of the hotel and then asked him if he could wait and take us to the first company where we had a meeting. He nodded that he could, and we were off.

Sinaia was even more beautiful than Bucharest, with cute chalets gleaming in the bright sunshine behind beautifully manicured lawns. The taxi headed into the old section of the city near the palace and stopped in front of a lovely little hotel painted a cheery yellow with white shutters.

The manager, Mihael, was very excited to have us as guests and settled us into our rooms very quickly so the cab wouldn't charge us extra. He shooed us out to the cab as soon as our luggage was dropped in the rooms.

I showed the cabbie the address for BAYtech, and he nodded his head. Turning the cab into traffic, he aimed it at the mountains, and we were soon climbing.

The company was located on a beautiful meadow at the edge of a great forest. It was securely surrounded by an imposing fencing that somehow artistically did not detract from the beauty of the location. The building itself looked ultra-modern and new. It was neither the old European romance style of architecture nor the utilitarian style of the Communists that we had only seen here.

We were stopped at the guard gate, and the cab was forced to unload and exit. We paid the cab and showed our passports to the guard, who checked a clipboard he had inside the gate.

"Wait here," he ordered in English.

Soon, a large golf cart came down the drive from the building, and the gate opened. The cart stopped, and a handsome man in his twenties got out of the driver's seat. He shook each one of our hands with a huge grin on his face and introduced himself as Alexi, assistant to the chief of development.

We were soon loaded onto the cart and heading into the building. Alexi explained that BAYtech was a technology company that specialized in sound tech. He ushered us to a conference room and brought in a big tray of coffee for us. The BAYtech team immediately joined us, and my jaw promptly hit the conference room table.

Their team was composed of three members, each one more attractive than the other. They were stunningly handsome. The head guy, Stefan, was in his thirties, and his two assistants were in their twenties. Stefan was tall with dark hair slicked back over shaved sides, which I had already seen was the Romanian style. He had dark eyes that were constantly watching and seemed very brash. Lucian, one of the assistants, was losing his hair, so it was cut short. He had a full blond beard and mustache under beautiful blue eyes. Fane also had his head shaved except the top, which was very long. He had slickly pulled it back into a very small ponytail that hung above his shaved head at the back. He had brown facial hair and warm chocolate eyes that were at once arresting and welcoming.

"Gentlemen, we are so happy to have you here at BAYtech," Stefan greeted us.

We stood and shook each of their hands as he introduced his team. I introduced our team, and we all had a seat. Stefan explained that Fane and Lucian did not speak English, so I asked Florian to interpret for them.

"There will be no need," Stefan said. "We have developed a translation app for your cell phone. They will simply plug in to understand." He said something in Romanian, and the two men took out their cells and installed one earbud in one of their ears.

"Now, we are ready, yes?" Stefan asked.

"Yes," I answered.

He looked at me for a moment and then said, "Pardon my hesitation, but it is highly unusual for a marked man to be in your position, no?"

"I guess," I said with a slight shrug. "To be honest, I wasn't expecting to be in this position, but the head of our delegation is . . . under the weather."

"Yes, Mr. High seems to have gotten a bad piece of pastrami."

How the hell does he know that?

Almost as if he could read my mind, he answered my question by saying, "Romania is a small country, no?"

"Beautiful country. We are really enjoying our trip so far.

"Excellent. Well, let's get down to business, shall we?"

"Yes," I agreed.

ABOUT THE AUTHOR

This is Crawford's eighth book in his series, The Master & Servant — Batting Cage, Gridiron Cage, Celluloid Cage, Hardwood Cage, Ice Cage, Country Cage, Comic-Lined Cage, and Rusty Cage. Rusty Cage was inspired by a trip to the beach with old friends.

Crawford also writes The Romanian Chronicles series based on classic movie monster stories — The Dark Master, The Re-animated Master, The Pack Master, and The Mystic Master. He was inspired by a summer trip to Romania and Russia where he completed four books.

He looks forward to continuing to travel and publishing more books in each series.

www.ingramcontent.com/pod-product-compliance
Lightning Source LLC
Chambersburg PA
CBHW070832120626
46556CB00002B/728

* 9 7 8 1 4 8 7 4 2 6 4 3 9 *